Cathy Williams can remember reading Mills & Boon books as a teenager, and now that she is writing them she remains an avid fan. For her, there is nothing like creating romantic stories and engaging plots, and each and every book is a new adventure. Cathy lives in London. Her three daughters—Charlotte, Olivia and Emma—have always been, and continue to be, the greatest inspirations in her life.

THE TYCOON'S ULTIMATE CONQUEST

CATHY WILLIAMS

MILLS & BOON

First Published in Great Britain 2018
by Mills & Boon, an imprint of HarperCollins*Publishers*
1 London Bridge Street, London, SE1 9GF

 © 2018 Cathy Williams

ISBN: 978-0-263-07696-7

MIX
Paper from
responsible sources
FSC **FSC™ C007454**
www.fsc.org

This book is produced from independently certified FSC™ paper
to ensure responsible forest management.
For more information visit www.harpercollins.co.uk/green.

Printed and bound in Great Britain
by CPI Group (UK) Ltd, Croydon, CR0 4YY

CHAPTER ONE

'THERE'S A PROBLEM,' the middle-aged man sitting in the chair in front of Arturo da Costa stated without preamble.

Art sat back, linked his fingers on his stomach and looked at Harold Simpson, a man who was normally calm, measured and so good at his job that Art couldn't think of a time when *anything* had been a problem for him. He ran the vast legal department of Art's sprawling empire with impeccable efficiency.

So at the word *problem* Art frowned, already mentally rescheduling the meeting he was due to attend in half an hour as he anticipated a conversation he wasn't going to enjoy, about a situation he would not have foreseen and which would be tricky to resolve.

'Talk to me,' he said, his deep voice sharp, knowing Harold was a rare breed of man who wasn't intimidated by his clever and unashamedly arrogant and unpredictable boss.

'It's the development in Gloucester.'

'Why is there a problem? I've got all the necessary planning permission. Money's changed hands. Signatures have been put on dotted lines.'

'If only it were that simple.'

'I don't see what could possibly be complex about this, Harold.'

'I suppose *complex* wouldn't quite be the right word, Art. *Annoying* might be the description that better fits the bill.'

'Not following you.' Art leaned forward, frowning. 'Don't I pay you to take care of annoying problems?'

Harold deflected the direct hit with a reprimanding look and Art grinned.

'You've never come to me with an annoying problem before,' he drawled. 'Perhaps I was rash in assuming that you dealt with them before they could hit my desk.'

'It's a sit-in.'

'Come again?'

Instead of answering, Harold opened up his laptop and swivelled it so that it was facing his boss, then leaned away as if waiting for the reaction he was expecting, a reaction which would have sent strong men diving for cover.

Fury.

Art looked at the newspaper article staring him in the face. It was from a local paper, circulation circa next to nothing, read by no one who mattered and covering an area where sheep probably outnumbered humans, but he could immediately see the repercussions of what he was reading.

His mouth tightened and he reread the article, taking his time. Then he looked at the grainy black-and-white picture accompanying the article. A sit-in. Protestors. Placards. Lots of moral high ground about the wicked, cruel developers who planned to rape and pillage the countryside. *Him*, in other words.

'Has this only now come to your attention?' He sat back and stared off into the distance with a thoughtful frown, his sharp mind already seeking ways of diverting the headache staring him in the face and coming up with roadblocks.

'It's been simmering,' Harold said as he shut the lid of his computer, 'but I thought I could contain the situation. Unfortunately, the lawyer working on behalf of the protesters has got the bit between her teeth, so to speak, and is determined to put as many obstacles in the way of your development as she can. Trouble is, in a small community like that, even if she loses the case and of course she will because, as you say, all the crosses have been made in the right boxes, the fallout could still be…unfortunate.'

'I admire your use of understatement, Harold.'

'She can rally the community behind her and the luxury development that should, in normal circumstances, sell in a heartbeat with the new train link due to open a handful of miles away, could find itself sticking on the open market. She's anti building on green fields and she's going to fight her corner, win or lose and come what may. Expensive people moving into expensive houses like to fancy themselves as mucking in with the locals and eventually becoming pillars of the community. They wouldn't like the prospect of the locals going quiet every time they walk into the village pub and pelting eggs against their walls in the dead of night.'

'I had no idea you had such impressive flights of fancy, Harold.' Art was amused but there was enough truth in what his lawyer had said to make him think. 'When you say *she*...?'

'Rose Tremain.'

'Miss... Mrs...or Ms?'

'Very definitely *Ms.*'

'I'm getting the picture loud and clear. And on the subject of pictures, do you have one of her? Is she floating around somewhere on the World Wide Web?'

'She disapproves of social media insofar as it personally pertains to *her*,' Harold said with a trace of admiration in his voice that made Art's eyebrows shoot up. 'No social media accounts...nothing of the sort. I know because I got one of my people to try to find out how we could follow her, try to get a broader picture of her, but no luck. There's the bones of past cases but no personal information to speak of at all. It would appear that she's old-fashioned like that.'

'There's another word for it,' Art drawled drily.

'I've only had dealings with her over the phone so far, and of course by email. I could give you my personal impressions...'

'I'm all ears.'

'Can't be bought off,' Harold said bluntly, instantly killing Art's first line of attack.

'Everyone has a price,' he murmured without skipping a beat. 'Have you any pictures of her at all?'

'Just something in one of the articles printed last week about the development.'

'Let's have a look.' Art waited, thinking, as Harold

expertly paged through documents in his pile of folders before eventually showing him an unsatisfactory picture of the woman in question.

Art stared. She *looked* like a *Ms.* The sort of feminist hippy whose mission might be to save the world from itself. The newspaper article showed him a picture of the sit-in, protesters on his land with placards and enough paraphernalia to convince him that they weren't going anywhere any time soon. All that was missing was a post office and a corner shop, but then summer was the perfect time for an impromptu camping expedition. He doubted they would have been quite as determined if those fields had been knee-deep in snow and the branches of the trees bending at ninety-degree angles in high winds.

Whatever the dark-haired harridan had said to them to stoke up public outrage at his development, she had succeeded because the untidy lot in the picture looked as self-righteous as she did.

The picture he was now staring at, of *Ms Rose Tremain*, showed a woman jabbing her finger at someone out of sight, some poor sod unfortunate enough to be asking her to answer a few questions she didn't like. Her unruly hair was scraped back into *something*, leaving flyaway strands around her face. Her clothes beggared belief. Art was accustomed to dating women who graced catwalks, women who were best friends with cutting-edge designers and spent whatever time they had away from their modelling jobs in exclusive salons beautifying themselves.

He squinted at the picture in front of him and tried to

get his head around the image of someone who looked as though she had bulk-bought her outfit from a charity shop and hadn't been near a hairdresser in decades.

No. Money wasn't going to get her off his back. One look at that jabbing finger and fierce scowl was enough to convince him of the rashness of going down that road.

But there were many ways to skin a cat...

'So, she can't be bought,' Art murmured, half to himself. 'Well, I will have to find another way to convince her to drop her case against me and get those protestors off my land. Every day lost is costing me money.' With his dark eyes still on the picture in front of him, Art connected to his PA and told her to reschedule his calendar for the next fortnight.

'What are you going to do?' Harold asked, sounding alarmed, as if he couldn't make sense of his workaholic boss taking two weeks off.

'I'm going to take a little holiday,' Art said with a slow smile of intent. 'A busman's holiday. You will be the only one privy to this information, so keep it to yourself, Harold. If *Ms Tremain* can't be persuaded to my way of thinking by a generous contribution to whatever hare-brained "Save the Whale" cause she espouses, then I'm going to have to find another way to persuade her.'

'How? If we're talking about anything illegal here, Art...'

'Oh, please.' Art burst out laughing. 'Illegal?'

'Maybe I don't mean *illegal*. Maybe a better word might be *unethical*.'

'Well, now, my friend. That depends entirely on your definition of unethical...'

* * *

'Someone here to see you, Rose.'

Rose looked up at the spiky-haired young girl standing by the door of the office she shared with her co-worker, Phil. It was little more than a large room on the ground floor of the Victorian house which was also her home but it was an arrangement that worked. The rent she got from Phil and from the occupants of the other two converted rooms—who were variously the local gardening club twice a week, the local bridge group once a week and the local children's playgroup twice a week—covered the extensive running costs of the house she had inherited when her mother had died five years previously. Well, alongside the sizeable loan she had had to take out in order to effect urgent repairs on the place.

She occasionally thought that it would have been nice if she could have separated her work life from her home life but, on the other hand, who could complain about a job where there was no commute involved?

'Who is it, Angie?' Bad time. Middle of the afternoon and she still had a bucketload of work to do. Three cases had cropped up at precisely the same time and each one of them involved complex issues with employment law, in which she specialised, and demanded a lot of attention.

'Someone about the land.'

'Ah. The land.' Rose sat back, stretched and then stood up, only realising how much she'd cramped up when she heard a wayward joint creak.

The land.

No one called it anything else.

Between Phil's property law side of the business and her labour law, *the land* had become the middle ground which occupied them both, far more than either had expected when the business of some faceless tycoon buying up their green fields to build yet another housing estate had reared its ugly head.

Phil was a relative newcomer to the area, but she had lived in the village her whole life and she had adopted the cause of the protestors with gusto.

Indeed, she had even allowed them to use her sprawling kitchen as their headquarters.

She was unashamedly partisan and was proud of her stance. There was nothing that stuck in her throat more than big businesses and billionaire businessmen thinking that they could do as they pleased and steamroll over the little people so that they could make yet more money for themselves.

'Want me to handle it?' Phil asked, looking up from his desk, which was as chaotic as hers.

'No.' Rose smiled at him. She could never have hoped for a more reliable business partner than Phil. Thirty-three years old, he had the appearance of a slightly startled owl, with his wire-rimmed specs and his round face, but he was as sharp as a tack and won a breathtaking amount of business for them. 'If they've actually got around to sending one of their senior lawyers then I'm ready for them. It's insulting that so far they've only seen fit to send junior staff. Shows how confident they are of being able to trample us into the ground.'

'I like your faith in our ability to bring a massive corporation to its knees,' Phil said with a wry grin. 'DC Logistics pretty much owns the world.'

'Which,' Rose countered without skipping a beat, 'doesn't mean that they can add this little slice of land to the tally.'

She tucked strands of her unruly hair into the sort of bun she optimistically started each and every day with, only to give up because her hair had a will of its own.

She glanced at the sliver of mirror in between the bookshelves groaning under the weight of legal tomes and absently took in the reflection that stared back at her every morning when she woke up.

No one had ever accused her of being pretty. Rose had long accepted that she just wasn't, that she just didn't fit the mould of *pretty*. She had a strong, intelligent face with a firm jaw and a nose that bordered on sharp. Her large eyes were clear and brown and her best feature as far as she was concerned.

Everything else…well, everything else worked. She was a little too tall, a little too gangly and not nearly busty enough, but you couldn't concern yourself with stuff like that and she didn't. Pretty much.

'Right! Let's go see what they've thrown at us this time!' She winked at Phil and made approving noises when Angie said that she'd stuck their visitor in the kitchen—it would do whoever it was good to see the evidence of their commitment to the cause—and headed out of the office.

She didn't know what to expect.

Overweight, overfed, overpaid and over-confident. Someone at the height of his career, with all the trappings that an expensive top job afforded. Angie had given nothing away and wouldn't have. She was gay and paid not a scrap of attention to what members of the opposite sex looked like.

Rose was only twenty-eight herself but the young people who had been sent to argue the case had seemed so much younger than her.

She pushed open the kitchen door and then stood for a few moments in the doorway.

The man was standing with his back to her, staring out at the garden, which flowed seamlessly into open land, the only boundary between private and public being a strip of trees and a dishevelled hedge of sorts.

He was tall. Very tall. She was five eleven and she guessed that he would be somewhere in the region of six three.

And, from what she was seeing, he was well built. Muscular. Broad shoulders tapering to a narrow waist and legs that moulded perfectly to the faded jeans he was wearing.

What sort of lawyer was *this*?

Confused, Rose cleared her throat to give notice of her presence and the man turned around slowly.

'My secretary didn't tell me your name, Mr...'

'Frank.' The stranger took his time as he walked towards her, which annoyed Rose because this was her house and her kitchen and yet the man seemed to dominate the space and own it in a way she didn't care for.

'Well, Mr Frank. You're here about the land, I gather. If your company thinks that this ploy is going to work, then I hate to disappoint you but it won't.'

Alarmed because he had somehow managed to close the distance between them and was standing just a little too close for comfort, Rose sidestepped him to the kettle, only offering him something to drink seemingly as an afterthought.

'You can sit,' she said crisply. 'Just shove some of the papers out of the way.'

'What ploy?'

Rose watched as he looked at the placards in the making on the kitchen table, head politely inclined. After some consideration, he held up one and examined it in reflective silence before returning it to its original position on the table.

'What ploy?' he repeated.

'The lawyer-in-jeans ploy,' Rose said succinctly. She shot him a look of pure disdain, but only just managed to pull it off because the man was just so…so…crazily good-looking that her nervous system felt as though it had been put through a spin cycle and was all over the place.

He'd sat down but not in a lawyer-like manner, which was also annoying. He'd angled the pine chair, one of ten around the long rectangular table, and was sprawled in it, his long legs stretched right out in front of him, one ankle over the other. He looked effortlessly elegant and incredibly *cool* in his weathered jeans and faded polo shirt. Everything clung in a way that made her think that the entire outfit had been especially designed with him in mind.

She pushed the coffee over to him. He looked just the kind of guy to take his coffee black, no sugar.

'Does your company think that they can send someone who's dressed down for the day in the hope that we
might just soften our stance? Maybe be deluded into
thinking that he's not the stuffed shirt lawyer that he
actually is?' She narrowed her eyes and tried and failed
to imagine him as a stuffed shirt lawyer.

'Ah…' Mr Frank murmured. '*That* ploy.'

'Yes. *That* ploy. Well, it won't work. My team and I
are committed to the cause and you can tell your em-
ployers that we intend to fight this abhorrent and unnec-
essary development with every ounce of breath in us.'

'You overestimate my qualifications,' Mr Frank said
smoothly, sipping the coffee. 'Excellent coffee, by the
way. I'm no lawyer. But were I to be one, then I would
try very hard not to be a stuffed shirt one.'

'Not a lawyer? Then who the heck are you? Angie
said that you were here about the land.'

'Angie being the girl with the spiky hair and the
nose ring?'

'That's correct. She also happens to be an extremely
efficient secretary and a whizz at IT.'

'Well, she was certainly right in one respect. I *am*
here about the land. Here to join the noble cause.'

Art's plan had been simple. It had come to him in a
blinding flash shortly after Harold had informed him
that money wasn't going to make the problem of squat-
ters on his land go away.

If you can't lick 'em, join 'em.

Naturally he'd known what to expect but somehow,

in the flesh, the woman staring at him through narrowed eyes wasn't *quite* the hippy he had originally imagined.

He couldn't put his finger on what was different and then, in the space of a handful of seconds, decided that it was a case of imagination playing tricks because she was certainly dressed in just the sort of attire he'd expected. Some sort of loose trousers in an assortment of clashing colours. Practical, given the hot weather, but, in all other respects, frankly appalling. A shapeless green vest-like top and a pair of sandals that, like the trousers, were practical but ticked absolutely no other boxes as far as he was concerned.

Her hair seemed to be staging a full-scale revolt against its half-hearted restraints. It was very curly and strands of it waved around her cheeks.

But the woman emanated *presence* and that was something he couldn't deny.

She wasn't beautiful, not in the conventional sense of the word, but she was incredibly arresting and for a few seconds Art found himself in the novel situation of temporarily forgetting why he was sitting here in a kitchen that looked as though a bomb had recently been detonated in it.

And then it all came back. He would join the band of merry protestors. He would get to know the woman. He would convince her from the position of insider that she was fighting a losing battle.

He would bring her round to his way of thinking, which was simply a matter of bringing her round to common sense, because she was never going to win this war.

But strong-arm tactics weren't going to work because, as Harold had made perfectly clear, storming in and bludgeoning the opposition would be catastrophic in a community as tightly knit as this one clearly was.

He was simply going to persuade her into seeing his point of view and the best and only way he could do that would be from the inside, from the position of one of them. From the advantageous position of trust.

Art didn't need opposition. He needed to butter up the unruly mob because he had long-term plans for the land—plans that included sheltered accommodation for his autistic stepbrother, to whom he was deeply attached.

He hadn't gone straight to the site though, choosing instead to make himself known to the woman standing firmly between him and his plans. He was good with women. Women liked him. Quite a few positively adored him. And there weren't many who didn't fall for his charm. Art wasn't vain but he was realistic, so why not use that charm to work its magic on this recalcitrant woman?

If that failed to do the trick then of course he would have to go back to the drawing board, but it was worth a shot.

To this end, he had taken his unprecedented leave of absence. A few days to sort out urgent business that wouldn't happily sit on the back burner and now here he was.

He was sporting the beginnings of a beard, was letting his hair grow, and the sharp handmade suits had ceded to the faded jeans and a black polo shirt.

'Really?' Rose said with a certain amount of cynicism.

'Indeed. Why the suspicion?'

'Because you don't exactly fit the role of the protestors we have here.'

'Don't I? How so?'

'Basically, I have no idea who you are. I don't recognise you.'

'And you know everyone who's protesting?'

'Everyone and, in most cases, their extended families, as well. You're not from around here, are you?'

'Not quite,' Art murmured vaguely, unprepared for such a direct line of attack before he'd even started writing incendiary messages on a placard.

'Well, where *are* you from? Exactly?'

Art shrugged and shifted in his chair. He was beginning to understand why the deputies sent to do this job had failed. Right now, Rose was staring at him as though he was something suspect and possibly contagious that had somehow managed to infiltrate her space.

'Can anyone say *exactly* where they're from?' he threw the question back at her, which only made her look at him with even more suspicion.

'Yes. Everyone on the site, for a start. As for me, I'm from here and always have been, aside from a brief spell at university.'

'I largely live in London.' Which was technically accurate. He *did* largely live in London. In his penthouse in Belgravia. He was also to be found in five-star hotels around the world, several of which he owned, or in one of the many houses he owned, although those occasions were slightly rarer. Who had time to wind down in a villa by the sea?

Strangely, that non-answer seemed to satisfy her because she stopped looking as though she had her finger on the buzzer to call for instant backup. 'So what are you doing here?' she asked with curiosity. 'I mean, why this cause? If you're not from around here, then what does it matter to you whether the land is destroyed or not?'

'*Destroy* is a big word.' Art was outraged but he held onto his temper and looked at her with an expression of bland innocence.

Definitely arresting, he thought. Exotic eyes. Feline. And a sensuous mouth. Wide and expressive. And an air of sharp intelligence which, it had to be said, wasn't one of the foremost qualities he ever sought in a woman, but it certainly worked in this instance because he was finding it hard to keep his eyes off her.

Rose fidgeted. To her horror, she felt the slow crawl of colour stain her cheeks. The man was gazing at her with hooded eyes and that look was doing all sorts of unexpected things to her body.

'It's *exactly* the right word,' she snapped, more sharply than she had intended, a reaction to those dark, sexy eyes.

Never had she felt more self-conscious, more aware of her shortcomings. The comfortable and practical culottes, which were the mainstay of her wardrobe on hot summer days, were suddenly as flattering as a pair of curtains and the loose-fitting vest as attractive as a bin liner.

She reminded herself that she wasn't the star attraction in a fashion parade. Clothes did not the man, or woman, make!

But for the first time in living memory she had the crazy urge to be something other than the determined career lawyer who worked hard on behalf of the underdog. She had the crazy urge to be sexy and compelling and wanted for her body instead of her brain.

'Too many developers over the years have whittled away at the open land around here.' She refocused and brought her runaway mind back on track. 'They've come along and turned the fields, which have been enjoyed for centuries by ramblers and nature lovers, into first a stupid shopping mall and then into office blocks.'

Rose half expected him to jump in here and heatedly side with her but he remained silent and she wondered what was going through that impossibly good-looking head of his.

'And this lot?'

'DC Logistics?' She loosed a sarcastic laugh under her breath. 'The worst of the lot. Certainly the biggest! They want to construct a housing development. But then I don't suppose I'm telling you anything you don't already know. Which brings me back to my question—why the interest in joining our protest?'

'Sometimes—' Art played with the truth like a piece of moulding clay '—big, powerful developers need to understand the importance of working in harmony with nature or else leaving things as they stand and, as you say, DC Logistics is the mother of all big companies.'

He succeeded in not sounding proud of this fact. When he thought of the work that had gone into turning the dregs of what had been left of his father's companies, after five ex-wives had picked them over in outrageous alimony settlements, into the success story of today he was pretty proud of his achievements.

Art had lived through the nightmare of his father's mistakes, the marriages that had fallen apart within seconds of the ink on the marriage certificates being dry. He'd gritted his teeth, helpless, as each ex-wife had drained the coffers and then, after his father had died several years previously, he'd returned to try to save what little remained of the thriving empire Emilio da Costa had carefully built up over time.

Art had been a young man at the time, barely out of university but already determined to take what was left and build it again into the thriving concern it had once been when his mother—Emilio da Costa's first wife and only love—had been alive.

Art might have learned from the chaos of his father's life and the greed of the women he had foolishly married that love was for the birds, but he had also learned the value of compassion in his unexpected affection for his stepbrother, José—not flesh and blood, no, but his brother in every sense of the word, who had been robustly ignored by his avaricious mother. The land was integral to his plan to make a home for José—the reason for Art needing to shut this protest down as quickly and as quietly as possible.

'Yes, it is,' Rose concurred. 'So you're idealistic,' she carried on in an approving tone.

The last time Art had been idealistic had been when he'd believed in Santa Claus and the Tooth Fairy. Witnessing the self-serving venom camouflaged as *true love* that had littered his father's life right up until his death had taken whatever ideals he might have had and entombed them in a place more secure than a bank vault.

'Well, you're in the right place.' Rose gestured to the paraphernalia in the kitchen. 'Obviously I don't devote all of my time to this cause. I couldn't possibly, but I do try to touch base with the people out there on a daily basis.'

'What's your main line of work?'

'Employment law.' Rose smiled and, just like that, Art felt the breath knocked out of his body.

The woman was more than arresting. When she smiled she was...*bloody stunning.* He felt the familiar kick of his libido, but stronger and more urgent than ever. Two months without a woman, he thought, would do that to a red-blooded man with a healthy sex drive. Because this outspoken feminist was certainly, on no level, what he looked for in a woman. He didn't do argumentative and he definitely didn't do the *let's-hold-hands-and-save-the-world* type. He did blondes. Big blonde hair, big blue eyes and personalities that soothed rather than challenged.

Rose Tremain was about as soothing as a pit bull.

And yet... His eyes lingered and his inconvenient erection refused to go away. The blood surging in his veins was hot with a type of dark excitement he hadn't felt in a very long time. If ever.

'Come again?' He realised that she had said something.
'Your line of work? What is it?'

'I dabble.'

'Dabble in what?'

'How much time have you got to spare? Could take a while.'

'Could take a while covering your many talents? Well, you're far from modest, aren't you?' She raised her eyebrows, amused and mocking, and Art smiled back slowly—deliberately slowly.

'I've never been a believer in false modesty. Sign of a hypocritical mind. I prefer to recognise my talents as well as my...er...shortcomings.'

'Well, whatever you do is your business—' she shrugged and stood up '—but if you're good at everything, which seems to be what you're implying, then you're going to be very useful to us.'

'How so?' Art followed suit and stood up, towering over her even though she was tall. 'Useful in what respect?'

'Odd jobs. Nothing major so no need to sound alarmed.' She looked around the kitchen. 'Everyone lends a helping hand when they're here. It's not just a case of people painting slogans on bits of cardboard with felt tip pens. Yes, we're all protesting for the same reason, but this is a small, close community. The guys who come here do all sorts of jobs around the house. They know I'm representing them for free and they're all keen to repay the favour by doing practical things in return. There are a couple of plumbers behind us and an electrician, and without them I have no idea how much money I would have had to spend to get some vital jobs on the house done.'

'So this is your house?' Art thought that it was a bit hypocritical, clamouring about rich businessmen who wanted to destroy the precious space around her so that they could line their evil pockets when she, judging from the size of the house, was no pauper.

Accustomed to storing up information that might prove useful down the line, he sensed that that was a conversation he would have in due course.

'It is, not that that's relevant,' Rose said coolly. 'What *is* relevant is that most of the town is behind us, aside from the local council, who have seen fit to grant planning permission. I've managed to really rally a great deal of people to support our cause and they've all been brilliant. So if you're a jack-of-all-trades then I'm sure I'll be able to find loads of practical ways you can help, aside from joining the sit-in, of course. Now, shall I take you to the scene of the crime…?'

CHAPTER TWO

'YOU HAVE A nice house,' Art commented neutrally as they exited the cluttered kitchen, out into the main body of the house which was equally cluttered. 'Big. You rent out rooms, I take it?' He detoured to push open the door to one of the huge ground-floor rooms and was confronted with an elderly man holding court with an image of a bunch of flowers behind him on the wall. The image was faded and unsteady because the projector was probably a relic from the last century. Everyone turned to stare at Art and he saluted briskly before gently shutting the door.

'If it's all the same to you, Mr Frank, I'll ask the questions. And please refrain from exploring the house because, yes, other organisations do avail themselves of some of the rooms and I very much doubt they want you poking your head in to say hello. Unless, of course, you have something to impart on the subject of orchid-growing or maybe some pearls of wisdom you could share with one of our Citizens Advice Bureau volunteers?'

'I've never been into gardening,' Art contributed truthfully. He slanted his eyes across to Rose, who was walking tall next to him, her strides easily matching his as they headed to the front door. The walls of the house were awash with rousing, morale-boosting posters. Voices could be heard behind closed doors.

'You're missing out. It's a very restful pastime.'

Art chuckled quietly. He didn't do *restful*.

'Wait a minute.' She looked at him directly, hands on her hips, her brown eyes narrowed and shrewdly assessing. 'There's one little thing I forgot to mention and I'd better be upfront before we go any further.'

'What's that?'

'I don't know who you are. You're not from around here and I'm going to make it clear to you from the start that we don't welcome rabble-rousers.'

Stunned, Art stared at her in complete silence.

He was Arturo da Costa. A man feared and respected in the international business community. A man who could have anything he wanted at the snap of an imperious finger. Grown men thought twice before they said anything they felt might be misconstrued as offensive. When he spoke, people inclined their heads and listened. When he entered a room, silence fell.

And here he was being accused of being a potential *rabble-rouser*!

'Rabble-rouser,' he framed in a slow, incredulous voice.

'It's been known.' She spun around on her heel, headed to the door and then out towards a battered navy blue Land Rover. 'Idlers who drift from one protest site to another, stirring up trouble for their own political motives.'

'Idlers…' Art played with the word on his tongue,

shocked and yet helpless to voice his outrage given he was supposed to be someone of no fixed address, there to support the noble cause.

'Granted, not all are idlers.' Rose swung herself into the driver's seat and slammed the door behind her, waiting for him to join her. She switched on the engine but then turned to him, one hand on the gearbox, the other on the steering wheel. 'But a lot of them are career protestors and I can tell you straight away that we don't welcome that lot. We're peaceful. We want our voices to be heard and the message we want to get across is not one that would benefit from thug tactics.'

'I have never been accused of being a rabble-rouser in my life before, far less a thug. Or an *idler*…'

'There's no need to look so shocked.' She smiled and pushed some of her curly hair away from her face. 'These things happen in the big, bad world.'

'Oh, I know all about what happens in the big, bad world,' Mr Frank murmured softly and the hairs on the back of her neck stood on end because his deep, velvety voice was as seductive as the darkest of chocolate.

In the sultry heat of the Land Rover, she could almost breathe him in and it was going to her head like incense.

'And before you launch into another outrageous accusation—' he laughed '—something along the lines that I don't know about the big, bad world because I'm a criminal, I'll tell you straight away that I have never, and will never, operate on the wrong side of the law.'

'I wasn't about to accuse you of being a criminal.' Rose blinked and cleared her throat. 'Although, of course,' she added grudgingly, 'I might have got round to that sooner or later. You can't be too careful. You should roll your window down. It'll be a furnace in here otherwise.'

'No air conditioning?'

'This relic barely goes,' she said affectionately before swinging around to expertly manoeuvre the courtyard which was strewn with cars, all parked, it would seem, with reckless abandon. 'If I tried to stick air conditioning in it would probably collapse from the shock of being dragged into the twentieth century.'

'You could always get a new car.'

'For someone who dabbles in a bit of this and that, you seem to think that money grows on trees,' she said tartly. 'If I ever win the lottery I might consider replacing my car but, until then, I work with the old girl and hope for the best.'

'Lawyers,' he said with a vague wave of his hand. 'Aren't you all made of money?'

Rose laughed and shot him a sideways look. He was slouched against the passenger door, his big body angled so that he could look at her, and she wondered how many women had had those sexy dark eyes focused on them, how many had lost their head drowning in the depths.

She fancied herself as anything but the romantic sort, but there was a little voice playing in her head, warning her that this was a man she should be careful of.

Rose nearly laughed because her last brush with romance had left a nasty taste in her mouth. Jack Shaw had been a fellow lawyer and she had met him on one of her cases, which had taken her to Surrey and the play-ground of the rich and famous. He had been fighting the corner for the little guy and she had really thought that they were on the same wavelength—and they should have been. He'd ticked all the right boxes! But for the second time in her adult life she had embarked on a relationship that had started off with promise only to end in disappointment. How was it possible for something that made sense to end up with two people not actually hav-ing anything left to say to one another after ten months?

Rose knew what worked and what didn't when it came to emotions. She had learned from bitter child-hood experience what to avoid. She knew what was un-suitable. And yet her two suitable boyfriends, with their excellent socialist credentials, had crashed and burned.

At this rate, she was ready to give up the whole find-ing love game and sink her energies into worthwhile causes instead.

'Not all lawyers are rich,' she said without looking at him, busy focusing on the road, which was lined with dense hedges, winding and very narrow. 'I'm not.'

'Why is that?'

'Maybe I chose the wrong branch of law.' She shrugged. 'Employment law generally doesn't do it when it comes to earning vast sums of money. Not that I'm complaining. I get by nicely, especially when you think about all the perfectly smart people who can't find work.'

'There's always work available for perfectly smart people.'

'Is that your experience?' She flashed him a wry

sidelong glance before turning her attention back to the road. 'Are you one of those perfectly smart people who finds it so easy to get work that you're currently drifting out here to join a cause in which you have no personal interest?'

'You're still suspicious of my motives?'

'I'm reserving judgement. Although—' she sighed '—I can, of course, understand how easy it is to get involved if you're a nature-lover. Look around you at the open land. You can really breathe out here. The thought of it being handed over to a developer, so that houses can be put up and the trees chopped down, doesn't bear thinking about.'

Art looked around him. There certainly was a great deal of open land. It stretched all around them, relentless and monotonous, acres upon acres upon acres of never-ending sameness. He'd never been much of a country man. He liked the frenetic buzz of city life, the feeling of being surrounded by activity. He made some appreciative noises under his breath and narrowed his eyes against the glare as the perimeters of his land took shape.

'So you've lived here all your life,' Art murmured as she slowed right down to access the bumpy track that followed the outer reaches of his property. 'I'm taking it that some of the guys protesting are relatives? Brothers? Sisters? Cousins? Maybe your parents?'

'No,' Rose said shortly.

Art pricked up his ears, detecting something behind that abrupt response. It paid to know your quarry and

Harold had been spot on when he'd said that there was next to no personal information circulating out there about the prickly woman next to him. Amazing. Social media was the staple diet of most people under the age of thirty-five and yet this woman had obviously managed to turn her back firmly on the trend.

Since he was similarly private about his life, he had to concede some reluctant admiration for her stance.

'No extended family?'

'Why the Spanish Inquisition?' She glanced across at him. 'What about *you*? Brothers? Sisters? Cousins? Will some of *your* extended family be showing up here to support us?'

'You're very prickly.'

'I…don't mean to be, Mr Frank.'

'I think we should move onto a first name basis. That okay with you? My name's Arturo. Arthur if you prefer the English equivalent.' Which was as close to the truth as it was possible to get, as was the surname, which hadn't been plucked from thin air but which was, in fact, his mother's maiden name.

'Rose.'

'And you were telling me that you weren't prickly…'

'I'm afraid the whole business of an extended family is something of a sore point with me.' She half smiled because her history was no deep, dark secret, at least locally. If Arthur, or Arturo because he looked a lot more like an exotic Arturo than a boring Arthur, ended up here for the long haul, then sooner or later he would hear the gossip. The truth was that her background had made her what she was, for which she was very glad, but it wasn't exactly normal and for some reason explaining herself to this man felt…awkward and a little intimate.

Aside from that, what was with the questioning? Shouldn't he be asking questions about the land instead of about *her*?

On a number of levels he certainly didn't respond in the predicted manner and again Rose felt that shiver, the faintly thrilling feathery sensation of being in slightly unchartered territory.

'You asked about me,' he said smoothly, filling the silence which had descended between them, 'and extended family is a sore point for me, as well. I have none.'

'No?' They had arrived at the protest site but Rose found that she wanted to prolong the conversation.

'Do you feel sorry for me?' Arturo grinned and Rose blinked, disconcerted by the stupendous charm behind that crooked smile. She felt it again, a whoosh that swept through her, making her breath quicken and her stomach swoop.

'Should I? You don't strike me as the sort of guy someone should be feeling sorry for. How is it that you have no extended family?'

'First, I'll take it as a compliment that you think I'm the kind of dominant guy people should fear, respect and admire instead of pity…'

'Did I say that?' But her mouth twitched with amusement.

'And, second, I'll tell you if you tell me. We can hold hands and have a girly evening sharing confidences…join me for dinner later. I'd love to get to know you better.'

Hot, flustered and suddenly out of her depth, Rose gaped at him like a stranded fish, scarcely believing her ears. She reddened, lost for words.

'Is it a promising start that I'm taking your breath away?' Arturo drawled, his voice rich with amusement.

'No... I... You're asking me on *a date*?'

'You sound as though it's something that's never happened to you before.'

'I...no... I'm very sorry, Mr Frank, but I...no. I can't accept. But thank you very much. I'm flattered.'

'Arturo.' He frowned. 'Why not?'

'Because...' Rose smoothed her wayward hair with her hand and stared off into the distance, all the while acutely aware of his dark, sexy eyes on her profile, making a nonsense of her level head and feet-firmly-planted-on-the-ground approach to life. She was no frothy, giggly bit of fluff but he was making her feel a bit like that and anyone would think that she was a giddy virgin in the company of a prince!

'Because...?'

'Well, it's not appropriate.'

'Why not? I may be about to join your cause, but you're not my boss so no conflict of interest there.'

'I...' Rose licked her lips and eventually looked at him, leaning against the open window. 'I...'

'You're not married. You're not wearing a wedding ring.'

'Observant. That's hardly the point, though.'

'Boyfriend?'

'No...not that it's any of your business, Mr Frank.

Arthur. *Arturo.* Do you usually ask women you've only known for five seconds out on a date?'

'How else am I supposed to get to know them for longer than five seconds if I don't? So you're not married, no boyfriend…gay?'

'No!'

Arturo grinned and Rose was certain she was blushing furiously, her reddened cheeks thoroughly letting the side down. 'Then where's the problem?'

'You're very sure of yourself, aren't you?' Rose gathered herself and opened her door. It was very hot. A blazing summer afternoon, with the sun still high in the sky and the clouds little more than cotton wool puffs of white idly floating by. The land looked glorious and untouched. It was a short walk to get to the site where the protestors had set up camp. Yes, she could have driven there, but it was easier to park here and a nice day for walking. Except now she would be walking in a state of nervous tension.

'Is that a crime?' Arturo had followed her out and he looked at her, still grinning.

'I've never been attracted to men who are too sure of themselves.'

'Challenging observation…'

'That's not my intention! You're here to…support us! And I won't be going out with you because… I'm not interested in any sort of relationship at this point in time.'

'Who's talking about a relationship?'

'I don't do casual sex.' Rose was staggered that she was having this conversation, but she had yet to meet a man who was open about what he wanted and surely

he couldn't want *her* because, rich or poor, he had the
sort of charisma and good looks that would guarantee
him a spot in any woman's little black book.

So why her?

But heck, was she flattered? It had been a while since
her last disastrous relationship, a while since she had
felt like a woman. And, if she was honest, even Jack,
earnest and brimming over with admirable integrity,
hadn't made her feel like this.

'I thought I just mentioned having dinner,' Arturo
murmured, which made Rose feel her cheeks flush what
was surely an even deeper shade of red.

'You're playing with me,' she said sharply. 'And I
don't like it.'

Their eyes tangled but Rose refused to be the first
to back down even though she wanted to.

Art was learning what it felt like to be politely but
firmly pushed to the kerb.

'Tell me about the protest,' he encouraged, changing
tack, matching her gait with his and releasing her from
the stranglehold of her embarrassment as they continued to walk towards the distant horizon. 'How many
people are there at the site?'

'Ever been on a protest before?'

'I can honestly say that I haven't.'

'Well, I'm glad that this is of sufficient interest to
you to get you motivated into doing more than just sitting on the sidelines and sympathising. So many people
have strong views about something and yet they never

quite go the distance when it comes to doing something about those views.'

'What made you choose employment law over something better paid?'

'Because money isn't everything! And I'm taking it that you feel the same as I do.'

'Money *can* often be the root of all evil,' Art hedged. 'It's also pretty vital when it comes to putting food on our plates.'

'I like to think that in my job I'm helping other people put food on their plates.'

'And you've always worked for yourself or did you work for a bigger company after you graduated?'

'You ask a lot of questions, don't you?' But she seemed flattered by his interest.

'It's the only way to get to know someone.' Art had the grace to flush. He was here for a purpose though and with him the practical would always take precedence over any unruly conscience. Vast sums of money were at stake and he was only trying to make his point of view known to a group who probably thought that their opinion was the only valid one on the table.

A rich diversity of opinion was a bonus in life. By *subtly* introducing a different viewpoint to theirs, he would effectively be doing her and all of the protestors there a laudable favour.

'Nearly twenty-five,' Rose told him briskly, walking fast, each stride determined and sure-footed.

'Nearly twenty-five what?'

'You asked how many protestors there were on the site. Nearly twenty-five and growing by the day.'

'And what lovely days we've been having...'

'They'd be here come rain or shine,' Rose informed him tartly and he grinned at her.

'And quite right too. Nothing worse than a protestor who packs up his placards and heads for his car the minute the skies open.'

'I can't tell when you're joking,' Rose said, pausing to look at him.

'Oh, I'm very serious about being here indeed. Make no mistake about that,' Art said softly.

'And how long do you plan on staying?' She began walking again and he fell in beside her.

'I reckon at least a few days, maybe longer. Perhaps a week or two.'

'Getting first-hand experience of putting your money where your mouth is.' Rose smiled. 'I commend that. The camp's just up ahead. We've managed to get running water and electricity going. It's been a nightmare but where there's a will there's a way and, like I said, there are a lot of people with a lot of talent who have been keen to help us out.'

Art was looking at a collection of makeshift dwellings. Tents rubbed shoulders with slightly more solid constructions. There was an elaborate portable toilet. People were milling around. Children were playing. It was, he had to concede, a wonderful campsite, dissected by a clear, bubbling stream and surrounded by trees and flowers. It was, however, a campsite on *his* land.

Clearly much loved and admired, the second they were spotted, Rose was surrounded by people, young and old alike. She was part and parcel of the community and Art could see the warmth of the supporters surround her like a blanket, seemingly reaffirming her belief in what they were doing—saving the land for the locals. Several dragged her along to have a look at some new ideas for placards. One old guy involved her in an elaborate discussion about some legal technicality, which she handled with aplomb and a great show of interest, even though he could somehow tell that she was answering his questions automatically.

No one paid the slightest bit of attention to him.

He was introduced, of course, and he, likewise, was shown yet more placards to add to the already healthy supply in evidence.

'Very artistic,' he contributed to one of the middle-aged women who had carted him off to one side. 'I like the...er...'

'Drawings?' She delightedly pointed to the illustration of stick figures holding placards showing stick figures holding placards. 'I'm trying to convey the idea that all of this is a never-ending problem which will just keep recurring until everyone feels as passionately about the countryside as we do.'

'Very imaginative.'

'I guess you'll be helping? Rose says you're interested in what's taking place in this little pocket of the world.'

'Very interested,' Art said with heartfelt honesty, relieved to be dragged away before he could be quizzed further. The woman struck him as the sort who took no prisoners.

Overhead, the sun continued to beat down with fe-

rocity. He felt hot and sweaty and in need of just a handful of those minor luxuries he took for granted. A nice
cool shower, for one thing.

He'd brought the minimum of clothes, stuffed into
a holdall which he'd left in the Land Rover. They nes-
tled on top of his computer, because there was no way
he intended to be completely out of reach. That would
have been unthinkable.

'So,' Rose said brightly when she was back at his
side, having done the rounds, including squatting on
the ground to talk to some of the children, 'I notice that
you didn't think to bring a tent.'

'Come again?'

'I'm getting ahead of myself.' She drew him to one
side. 'You said that you planned on staying for a few
days and you don't have a tent, but I think it might be
possible for you to share one. I know Rob over there
has a tent that's as big as a house and I'm sure he'd be
delighted to share his space with a fellow protestor.'

Art tried not to recoil with horror. 'That,' he all but
choked, 'won't do.'

'Why not?'

'Because I have some savings and I will dip into
them to stay somewhere…er…locally…'

'But why? Honestly, the site is really very comfortable. Everyone enjoys staying there.'

'And I applaud them, but that's not for me.'

'It's stupid to use your savings to rent somewhere
for a week. Or however long you plan on staying. Besides, in case you haven't noticed, this is an extremely
touristy part of the country. Dead in winter but the ho-

tels around here are expensive and almost all of them will be fully booked in summer.' She stood back and looked at him narrowly.

'I believe you when you say that you don't have criminal tendencies.' She folded her arms and inclined her head to one side.

'I'm breathing a sigh of relief as I stand here.'

'And I think it's ridiculous for you to waste your money trying to find somewhere around here to rent. You'll be broke by the end of a week. Trust me.' She said nothing for a few minutes, giving him ample time to try to figure out where this was heading.

But she didn't expand, instead choosing to begin walking back to the Land Rover, which was a long-winded exercise because she was stopped by someone every couple of steps. On the way she collected an offering of several files, which she promised to look at later.

'Nothing to do with the land,' she confided to Art when they were finally back in the muddy four-wheel drive and she was swinging away from the land, back out to the open road. 'George is having issues with one of his employees. Wants some advice. Normally it's the other way round for me, but I promised I'd have a look at the file.'

'Generous of you. I can see how popular you are with everyone there.'

Rose laughed, a musical sound of amusement that did the same thing to Art as her smile did, rousing him in ways that were unexpected and surprisingly intense.

He did know that there were pertinent questions he should be asking to further his understanding of how he could win this war without losing the battle but he couldn't seem to get his head in the right place to ask the right questions. Instead, he found himself staring at her from under his lashes, vaguely wondering what it was about her that was so compelling.

'Now that you've turned down my dinner invitation,' he drawled, 'perhaps you could drive me to the nearest, cheapest B&B. I'm touched at your concern for the level of my savings, but I'll manage.'

'There's no reason why you can't stay at my place.'

'Your place?'

Rose laughed, caught his eye sideways and forced a grin out of him. 'It's big and you can pay your way doing things around the house while you're there. Two of the rooms need painting, which is a job I never seem to get round to doing, and there's a stubborn leak in the tap. A constant drip, drip, drip.'

'You want me to fix leaks and paint your house?' DIY and Art had never crossed paths. Paint a room? Fix a leak? He couldn't have flung himself further out of his comfort zone if he'd tried.

'In return for free board and lodging. Oh, how good are you at cooking?'

'It's something I've always tried to avoid.'

'Do we have a deal?'

'Why do you live in such a big house if you can't afford to?'

'Long story.'

'I'm a very good listener. There's nothing I enjoy more than a long story. I guess we can get to that in due course because I would love to accept your generous offer.' He wondered what other skills she thought he possessed. There was a chance they would both end up in Casualty if he tried his hand at cooking, so he disabused her straight away on that count and she laughed and shrugged and laughed again and told him that it had been worth a shot.

'I can cook and when I put my mind to it I actually enjoy it, but I'm so busy all of the time that it always feels like a chore.'

'You might regret asking me to paint a room,' Art said seriously as she bumped along the narrow lanes, driving past clusters of picturesque houses with neat box hedges before the open fields swallowed them up again, only to disgorge them into yet another picturesque village. 'I'm very happy to try my hand at it, but one thing I do insist on doing is paying you for my accommodation.'

'Don't be stupid.'

'If you don't agree to this then you can dump me off right here and I'll sort myself out, whatever the cost.'

Rose clicked her tongue impatiently.

'You obviously need the money,' Art continued almost gently, as the outskirts of the village loomed into view. 'You rent rooms out and the place, from all accounts, is falling apart at the seams...'

'Very well.' She kept her eyes firmly focused on the road ahead. 'In which case, I'll accept your dinner invitation on the proviso that I cook dinner for you.'

'Deal,' Art drawled, relaxing back into the passenger seat. Could he have hoped for a better outcome than this? No.

He was looking forward to this evening. The thorny business of going undercover to talk some sense into his opposition wasn't going to be the annoying uphill trek he had originally foreseen after all...

In fact...hand on heart, Art could honestly say that he was looking forward to this little break in his routine.

CHAPTER THREE

By THE TIME they were back at the house the clatter of people had been replaced by the peace of silence. The gardening club crew had departed, as had whoever else was renting one of the downstairs rooms. Phil popped out and Art watched as he and Rose huddled in a brief discussion.

While they talked in low voices, he took the opportunity to look around him.

It was a big house but crying out for attention. The paint was tired, the carpet on the stairs threadbare and the woodwork, in places, cracked or missing altogether.

He made himself at home peering into the now empty rooms and saw that they were sizeable and cluttered with hastily packed away bits and pieces.

It was impossible to get any real idea of what the house might once have looked like in grander times because every nook and cranny had been put to use. Work desks fitted into spaces where once sofas and chaises longues might have resided, and in the office where she worked books lined the walls from floor to ceiling.

'Finished looking around?'

Art turned to find that she had broken off from talking to Phil, who was heading out of the front door, briefcase in hand and a crumpled linen jacket shoved under his arm.

'Which of the rooms needs the paint job?' was his response.

'It's actually upstairs,' Rose said, steering him away from the hall and back towards the kitchen where, he noted, no one had seen fit to tidy the paraphernalia of protest. 'Now—' she stood, arms folded, head tilted to one side '—tell me what you thought of our little band of insurgents.'

'Well organised.' Art strolled towards one of the kitchen chairs and sat down. 'But I'm curious—how long do they intend to stay there and what is the end objective?'

'That's an odd question,' Rose mused thoughtfully. 'Does your contribution to the cause depend on an answer to that?'

'I have a strong streak of practicality.' Art wasn't lying when he said that. 'I'm interested in trying to find out if there's any real chance of you winning with your protests.'

Rose sighed. 'Perhaps not entirely,' she admitted, 'but I really hope we can make some kind of difference, perhaps get the company to rethink the scale of their project. They're eating up a lot of open land and there's no question that the end result will be a massive eyesore on the landscape.'

'Have you seen the plans?' Art asked curiously.

'Of course I have. It's all about houses for wealthy commuters.'

'The rail link, I suppose...'

'You're the only person who has actually taken time out to think this through,' Rose admitted. 'And you're not even from round here. I think everyone somehow hopes that this is a problem that will just go away if we can all just provide a united front. It's a relief to talk to someone who can see the pitfalls. Just strange that you should care so much, considering this has never been your home.'

'I have general concerns about the...er...country-side.' Art had the grace to flush. Yes, all was fair in love and war, and it wasn't as though this little deception was actually harming anyone, but the prick of his conscience was an uneasy reminder that playing fast and loose with the truth was a lie by any other name.

'Does that extend to other concerns?' Rose asked with interest.

'What do you mean?'

'Problems on a larger scale. Climate change. Damage to the rainforests. Fracking and the impact on the green belt.'

Art was used to women who were either career-driven—those with whom he came into contact in the course of his working life—or else women he dated. On the one hand, he conversed with his counterparts with absolute detachment, regardless of whether he picked up any vibes from them, any undercurrent of sexual interest. And then, when it came to the women he dated... well, that was sex, relaxation and pleasure, and in-depth conversations were not the name of the game. Quite honestly, he thought that the majority of them would have been bored rigid were he ever to sit them down and initiate a conversation about world affairs. If there was a world out there of smart, sassy women who had what it took to turn him on, then he'd passed them by.

Until now...

Because, against all odds, he was finding that this outspoken woman was a turn-on and he didn't know why. She should have been tiresome, but instead she was weirdly compelling.

'Doesn't everyone think about the bigger picture?'

'I like that,' Rose murmured. 'I really get it that you think about the bigger picture. But you surely must have some form of employment that enables you to take off when you want to, be it here or somewhere else...' She turned away and began rustling for something to cook.

'Let me order something in.' Art was uncomfortable with this.

'Order something in?' She looked at him incredulously.

'There's no need for you to prepare anything for me.'

'We both have to eat and it won't be fancy. Trust me.'

'Are you usually this welcoming to people who walk off the street into your house?'

'You're a one-off.' She smiled a little shyly. Yes, she had lots of contact with the opposite sex. Yes, there was Phil and a wide assortment of men she met on a daily basis, either because they lived locally and she bumped into them or in the course of her work. But this was different. This was a reminder of what it felt like to be with a man and she was enjoying the sensation.

Of course, she sternly reminded herself, it wasn't as though he was anything more than a nice guy who happened to share the same outlook on life as she did.

A nice guy who just so happened to be drop-dead gorgeous...

'A *one-off*...?' He looked at her with assessing eyes and Rose burst out laughing. He sounded piqued, as though someone had stuck a pin in his ego. In a flash of wonderment because he was simply nothing like any man she had ever met before, she gathered that he was piqued because she wasn't bowled over by him. Or at least because that was the impression she had given. She had turned down his dinner date, had rejected his offer to pay rent and had set him a number of tasks to complete, which was probably a first for a guy like him. He might not have money but he had style and an underlying aggressive sexual magnetism that most women would find irresistible.

Their eyes tangled and Rose felt her nipples pinch in raw sexual awareness, and the suddenness of its potency made her breath catch in her throat.

'That's the problem with living in a small community.' Rose laughed breathlessly, deflecting a moment of madness which had smacked of her being lonely, which she most certainly was not. 'You tend to know everyone. A new face is a rare occurrence.'

'Surely not.'

'Maybe not at this time of year,' she admitted, 'when the place is swarming with tourists, but a new face here for something other than the nice scenery and the quaint village atmosphere…that's a bit more unusual.'

'Why do you stay?' Art asked with what sounded like genuine curiosity. 'And, if that's the case, then surely you must find it a little dull?'

'No, I don't. I'm not just a statistic here, one of a million lawyers sweating to get by. Here, I can actually make a difference. And I don't know why I'm telling you any of this.'

'Because I'm a new face and you don't get to have conversations with people you haven't known since you were a kid?'

Rose flushed and looked at him defiantly. 'Not all of us are born to wander, which reminds me—you never told me how it is that you can afford to take time out to be here. Yes, you've said you do a bit of this and a bit of that but you're obviously not a labourer.'

'What makes you say that?'

'Your hands, for a start. Not calloused enough.'

'I'm not sure that's a compliment,' Art drawled, glancing at his hands. The last time he'd done anything really manual had been as a teenager when he'd had a summer job working on a building site. He recalled that his father had been going through divorce number three right about then.

'Office jobs?'

'You ask a lot of questions.'

'No more than you,' Rose pointed out and Art grinned at her, dark eyes never leaving her face.

He hadn't thought through the details of why he was

here and it hadn't occurred to him that his presence would be met with suspicion. He was having to revise his easy assumption that he could just show up, mumble something vague and get by without any questions.

'I've been known to sit behind a desk now and again. I confess I'm interested in the details of a sit-in, in what motivates people to give up their home comforts for a cause.'

'You're not a reporter, are you?'

'Would you object if I told you that I was?'

'No. The more coverage the better...'

'Well, sorry to disappoint but,' Art drawled with complete honesty, 'I personally can't stand the breed. Nosy and intrusive.'

'But excellent when it comes to getting a message out there to the wider public.'

'They're a fickle lot,' Art countered. 'You think that they're on your side and you usually open yourself up to inevitable disappointment. If you're going to make me dinner and you won't allow me to buy anything in, then the least I can do is help.'

'Okay. You can chop vegetables and tell me why you're interested in what's happening here.' Rose rummaged in the fridge and extracted a random assortment of vegetables, fetched a couple of chopping boards and nodded to Art to take his place alongside her. 'Asking questions is what I do for a living.' She smiled, not looking at him. 'So you'll have to excuse me if I'm asking you a lot of them.'

Art was busy looking at the bundle of onions and tomatoes neatly piled in front of him. He held the knife and began fumbling his way to something that only laughably resembled food preparation. He only realised that she had stopped what she had been doing and was staring at him when she said with amusement, 'You haven't got a clue, have you?'

'These bloody things are making my eyes sting.'

'They have a nasty habit of doing that,' Rose agreed. 'And you're in for a rough ride if you intend to take a couple of hours dicing them. By the way, you need to dice them a whole lot smaller.'

'You're having fun, aren't you?'

'I'm thinking you look like a man who doesn't know his way round a kitchen very well.'

'Like I said, cooking has never appealed.'

'Not even when you're relaxing with someone and just having fun preparing a meal together?'

'I don't go there,' Art said flatly. He gave the onion a jaundiced look and decided to attack the tomatoes, which seemed a safer bet. 'I don't do domestic.'

'You don't *do* domestic? What does that mean?'

'It means that I don't share those cosy moments you've just described.'

'Why not?' she asked lightly.

'I don't do personal questions either.'

Looking into the ancient mirrored tiles that lined the counter, Art noted her pink cheeks. He met her eyes to find her staring at him, her pink cheeks going even pinker. She looked away hurriedly to continue slicing and dicing. Strands of her wildly curly hair fell around her face and she blew some of them out of her eyes, blatantly making sure *not* to look in those mirrored squares in case she caught his eye again.

'You don't do cosy and domestic,' Rose said slowly, swivelling to lean against the counter, arms folded, eyes narrowed, 'and you don't do personal questions. So, if I'm joining the dots correctly, you don't invite women to ask you why you're not prepared to play happy families with them.'

'Something like that.' Art shrugged. He was sharp enough to realise that there was no way he would ever get her onside if he came across as the sort of unliberated dinosaur she would clearly despise.

'No cooking together...no watching telly entwined on a sofa...'

'I definitely do the *entwined* bit,' Art joked. Rose failed to return his smile.

'You don't want to encourage any woman to think you're going to be in it for the long haul because you're a commitment-phobe.'

'I could lie and tell you that you're way off target there,' Art drawled, holding her stare, 'but I won't do you the disservice.'

'I like that,' Rose said slowly, not taking her eyes off him.

'Which bit?'

'The honesty bit. In my line of work, I see a lot of scumbags who are happy to lie through their teeth to get what they want. It's laudable that you're at least honest when it comes to saying what you think.'

'You're giving me more credit than I'm due.' Art stopped what he was doing and let his eyes rove over her. Her skin was satiny smooth and make-up-free. 'I like the way you look,' he murmured. 'I like the fact that you're completely natural. No warpaint. No pressing need to clone yourself on the lines of a certain doll. Really works.'

Rose glanced at him and looked away hurriedly. Those dark eyes, she thought, could open a lot of boxes and kick-start a whole host of chain reactions and she might not know how to deal with them.

Rose wasn't ready for a relationship with anyone and she certainly wasn't up for grabs when it came to any man who was a commitment-phobe. *Thanks, but no thanks.* Enjoying this man's company was a wonderful distraction but anything more than that was not going to be on the table.

She had to shake herself mentally and laugh inwardly at her fanciful thoughts; it wasn't as though she was in danger of any advances from this passing stranger, who had been nothing but open and polite with her!

And even if he *had* made any suggestive remarks then she would, of course, knock him back regardless of whether he was a drop of excitement in her otherwise pleasantly predictable life.

She was careful. When it came to men, she didn't dive head first into the water because you never knew what was lurking under the surface.

With the electrifying feel of those dark eyes broodingly watching her, Rose breathed in deep and remembered all the life lessons from her past. Remembered her mother, who had gone off the rails when Rose's father

had died. She'd lost her love and she had worked her
way through her grief with catastrophic consequences,
flinging herself headlong into a series of doomed relationships. Rose had been a child at the time but she
could remember the carousel of inappropriate men and
the apprehension she had felt every time that doorbell
had sounded.

Then Alison Tremain had fallen in love—head over
heels in love—with a rich, louche member of the landed
gentry who had promised her everything she'd been
desperate to hear. God only knew what she'd been
thinking. She'd been hired to clean the exquisite Cots-
wold cottage owned by his parents, where he and twelve
other fast-living friends had been staying for a long
weekend. Had her mother really thought that it was
love? But he'd swept her off her feet and maybe, Rose
had later thought, when she had looked back at events
through adult eyes, his heart had been in the right place.

The two had hurtled towards one another for all the
wrong reasons. Rose's mother because she'd wanted
an anchor in her life. She'd been swimming against the
tide and had been on the verge of drowning and he had
given her something to hold onto and she hadn't looked
further than the wild promises he'd made.

And he...he'd wanted to rebel against restrictive
parents and Alison Tremain had been his passport to
asserting authority over a life that had been dictated
from birth. Their disapproval would underline his inde-
pendence, would prove that he could choose someone
outside the box and damn the consequences. Brimming over with left-wing principles, he would be able

to ditch the upper-crust background into which he had been born.

It had been a recipe for disaster from the word *go* and, for Rose, the personal disaster had started when her mother had dumped her with their neighbour: *'Just for a bit...just until I'm sorted...and then I'll come to fetch you, that's a promise.'*

Everyone had rallied around as she had found herself suddenly displaced—the benefit of a small community—but there had been many times when she had entered a room unexpectedly to be greeted by hushed whispers and covert, pitying looks.

Rose knew that things could have been a lot worse. She could have ended up in care. As it was, she spent nearly two years with the neighbours, whose daughter went to the same school as her.

Her mother had written and Rose had waited patiently but by the time a much-chastened Alison had returned to the village Rose had grown into a cautious young girl, conscious of the perils of letting her emotions rule her life.

She'd witnessed her mother going off the rails because of a broken heart and had lived through her disappearing and getting lost in a world, she later learned, of soft drugs and alcohol because Spencer Kurtis had been unable to cope with the daily demands of a life without money on tap. So much for his rebellion. He had eventually crawled back to the family pile and Alison Tremain had returned to village life, where it had taken her a further year to recover before she was properly back to the person she had once been.

Rose knew better than to ever allow her behaviour to be guided by emotion. Sensible choices resulted in a settled life. Her sensible choices when it came to men, all two of them, might not have worked out but that didn't mean that she was going to rethink her ground plan.

She also knew better than to trust any man with money and time had only served to consolidate that opinion.

Her mother had been strung along by a rich man and in the end he hadn't been able to tear himself away from his wealthy background. But, beyond the story of one insignificant person, Rose had seen how, time and again, the wealthy took what they wanted without any thought at all for the people they trampled over.

The community that had rallied around her was, over the years, being invaded because developers couldn't keep their hands away from the temptation to take what was there and turn it into money-making projects. Their little oasis in the Cotswolds was achingly pretty and was also close enough to Oxford to save it from being too unremittingly rural.

In a very real sense, Rose felt that she owed a duty to the small community that had embraced her when her mother had started acting erratically and that included saving it from the whims of rich developers.

She was, for the first time in her life, sorely tempted to explain all of this to the ridiculously good-looking guy who, she noted wryly, had completely abandoned all attempts at vegetable preparation and was now pushing himself away from the counter to hunt down whatever wine was in the fridge.

'I never know what's there,' Rose said, half turning. 'The fridge has ended up being fairly communal property. Once a week someone has a go at tossing out whatever has gone past its sell-by date and everyone more or less tries to replace what's been taken so that we never find ourselves short of essentials like milk.'

'Doesn't that bug you?'

'No. Why should it?'

'Maybe because this is your house and a man's house should be his castle? What's the point of a castle if you let down the ramparts every two seconds to welcome in invaders? Who go through your belongings like gannets? Is this wine common property? Who does it belong to?' He held up a cheap bottle of plonk, which was better than nothing.

'That's mine and on the subject of one's house being one's castle, I can't afford that luxury.' Rose wasn't looking at him as she delivered this observation. In the companionable peace of the kitchen it felt comfortable to chat and she realised that, yes, quite often she longed for the pleasure of having the house to herself. 'I'm just lucky that I have this place. It was given to my mum by…er…by a friend and when she died it was passed onto me…'

Arturo looked at her carefully, but his voice was casual enough when he next spoke.

'Generous gift,' he murmured. 'Boyfriend? Lover? That kind of friend?'

'Something like that.' Rose swivelled, took the wine from him and, having bunged all the vegetables and seasoning into a pan with some sauce, she edged towards the kitchen table, absently sweeping some of the papers away and stacking half-finished cardboard placards into a pile on the ground. 'You're doing it again.'

'Doing what?' Arturo sipped some wine and looked at her over the rim of the glass.

'Prying,' she said drily. 'Is that a habit of yours? No, don't answer that.' She raised her eyebrows and shot him a shrewd assessing look. 'You pry. I gathered that the second you started opening doors to rooms when you first arrived, wanting to find out what was going on where. Must be your nature.'

'Expertly summed up... I like to find things out. How else can anyone have an informed opinion unless they're in possession of all the facts?'

'You're very arrogant, aren't you?' But she laughed, seeing that as commendable in someone who felt passionate about what was happening in the world around him. Too many people were content to sit on the fence rather than take a stand. Digging deep and arriving at an informed opinion was what separated the doer from the thinker. 'I mean that if you don't encourage domesticity and you don't do much talking to women then it's unlikely you ask them many questions about what they think. So why,' she added, 'are you being so inquisitive with me?'

'Maybe because I've never met anyone like you before.'

'Is that a good thing?' Rose detected the breathless note in her voice with a shiver of alarm. She was mesmerised by the lazy smile that lightened the harsh beauty of his face.

'For me, it's…strangely exciting.'

Her eyelids fluttered and her breathing hitched and her whole body suddenly tingled as though she had been caressed.

Arturo looked at her with leisurely, assessing eyes. He was clearly used to having what he wanted when it came to women. She sensed it included immediate gratification.

'I… Look… I didn't ask you to stay here…because… because…' She cleared her throat and subsided into awkward silence.

'Of course not, but I'm not the only one feeling this thing, am I?'

'I don't know what you're talking about.'

'No? We'll run with that for the time being, shall we? Tell me about the house.'

Rose blinked. Somewhere along the line she'd stopped being the feisty lawyer with the social conscience and had morphed into…a gawky adolescent with a teenage crush on the cute new boy in class. The chemistry between them was overwhelming. It slammed into her like a fist and the fact that he felt it as well, felt *something* at any rate, only made the situation worse. She'd spent a lifetime protecting herself from her emotions getting the better of her, had approached men with wariness because she knew the sort of scars that could be inflicted when bad choices went horribly wrong. On no level could this man be described as anything but a bad choice. So why was she perspiring with nerves and frantically trying to shut down the slide show of what could happen if she gave in…?

'The house?' she parroted, a little dazed.

'You were telling me that you inherited the house… that your mother was given it…'

'Right.'

And how had that come about? she wondered. *When she was the last person who made a habit of blabbing about her personal life?*

Disoriented at the chaos of her thoughts, she set to finishing the meal—anything to tear her gaze away from his darkly compelling face—but her hand was shaking slightly as she began draining pasta and warming the sauce.

'My mother had a fling with a guy,' she said in a halting voice, breathing more evenly now that she wasn't gawping at him like a rabbit caught in the headlights.

'Happens…'

'Yes, it does.' She swung around to look him squarely in the eyes. 'Especially when you're in mourning for the man you thought you'd be sitting next to in your old age, watching telly and going misty-eyed over the great-grandchildren…'

'What do you mean?'

Rose sighed. 'Nothing.'

'Tell me more.' Art hadn't eaten home-cooked food in any kitchen with any woman for a very, very long time. He dug into the bowl of pasta with gusto, realising that he was a lot hungrier than he'd thought.

He was eating here, just a stranger passing through instead of a billionaire to be feared, feted and courted by everyone with whom he came into contact. This was what normality felt like. He could scarcely remember the feeling. He wondered whether this was why he was intensely curious about her because she, like this whole experience, represented something out of the ordinary. Or maybe, he decided, it just stemmed from the fact that no information he could glean from her would be put to waste, not when he had a job to do. This was all just part of the game and what else was life but an elaborate game? In which there would inevitably be winners and losers and when it came to winning Art was the leader of the pack.

Far more comfortable with that pragmatic explanation, Art shot her an encouraging look.

'It's no big deal.' Rose shrugged and twirled some spaghetti around her fork, not looking at him. 'My father died when I was quite young and for a while my mum went off the rails. Got involved with...well...it was—' she grimaced and blushed '—an interesting time all round. One of the guys she became involved with was a rich young minor aristocrat whose parents owned a massive property about ten miles away from here. It ended in tears but years later, out of the blue, she received this house in his will, much to everyone's surprise. He'd been handed swathes of properties on his twenty-fifth birthday and he left this house to Mum, never thinking he'd die in a motorbike accident when he was still quite young.'

'A tragedy with a fortunate outcome.' Art considered the parallels between their respective parents and felt a tug of admiration that she had clearly successfully navigated a troubled background. He had too, naturally, but he was as cold as ice and just as malleable. He had been an observant, together teenager and a controlled, utterly cool-headed adult. He'd also had the advantage of money, which had always been there whatever the efforts of his father's grasping ex-wives to deprive him of as much of it as they possibly could.

She, it would seem, was cut from the same cloth. When he thought of the sob stories some of his girl-friends had bored him with, he knew he'd somehow ended up summing up the fairer sex as hopeless when it came to dealing with anything that wasn't sunshine and roses.

'Guilty conscience,' Rose responded wryly. 'He really led my mother off the straight and narrow, and then dumped her for reasons that are just too long-winded to go into. Put it this way—' she neatly closed her knife and fork and propped her chin in the palm of her hand '—he introduced her to the wonderful world of drugs and drink and then ditched her because, in the end, he needed the family money a lot more than he needed her. He also loved the family money more than he could ever have loved *her*.'

'Charming,' Art murmured, his keen dark eyes pinned to the stubborn set of her wide mouth.

'Rich.'

'Come again?'

'He was rich so he figured he could do as he pleased and he did, not that it didn't work out just fine in the end. Mum…came home and picked up the pieces and she was a darn sight better off without that guy in her life.'

'Came home…? Picked up the pieces…?'

Rose flushed. 'She disappeared for a while,' she muttered, rising to clear the table.

'How long *a while*?'

'What does any of this have to do with the protest?'

'Like I told you, I'm a keen observer of human nature. I enjoy knowing what makes people tick…what makes them who they are.'

'I'm not a specimen on a petri dish,' she said with more of her usual spirit, and Art burst out laughing.

'You're not,' he concurred, 'which doesn't mean that I'm any the less curious. So talk to me. I don't do domestic and I don't do personal conversations but I'm sorely tempted to invite you to be the exception to my rule. My *one-off*, so to speak…'

CHAPTER FOUR

TELL ME MORE...

Art bided his time. Curiosity battled with common
sense. For some reason, over the next three days he
kept wanting to return to the story of her past. His ap-
petite to hear more had been whetted and it was all he
could do to stamp down the urge to corner her and pry.

But that wasn't going to do.

He hadn't pursued the subject three days previously
when his curiosity had been piqued because he had
known that playing the waiting game was going to be
a better bet.

He'd already gleaned one very important piece of
information. She needed money. And while she might
carry the banner of *money can't buy you happiness* and
the good things in life are free, Art knew that reality
had very sharp teeth.

The house was falling down around her and whilst
she did get some money from the tenants, enough to
cover the essentials, from what she had told him in
dribs and drabs she simply didn't earn enough to keep
things going.

And houses in this part of the world weren't cheap. He knew because he'd strolled through the village, taking in all the great little details that made it such a perfect place for an upmarket housing development.

He wondered whether he could offer her something tantalising to call off the protest. He might have to dump the fellow protestor guise and reveal his true identity or he could simply contrive to act as a middleman to broker a deal. At any rate, he played with the idea of contributing something towards the community, something close to her heart that would make her think twice about continuing a line of action that was never going to pay dividends. Harold had been right when he'd painted his doomsday picture of a close-knit, hostile community determined to fend off the rich intruders with their giant four-wheel drive wagons and their sense of entitlement. They'd be wrong but since when did right and wrong enter into the picture when emotions were running high?

And Art needed peace. He needed the community onside. He needed to get past this first stage of development to reach the important second stage. When he thought of the benefits of the equestrian and craft centre he hoped to develop, for his stepbrother and the small intake of similar adults like his stepbrother, he knew just how vital it was for him to win this war with the backing of the people waving the placards. If he barrelled through their protest with marching boots they would turn on him and all his long-term plans would lie in ruins.

He'd met all the people who were protesting and the majority of them had kids who attended the local school.

He could appeal to them directly, imply that the heartless developers might be forced to build a new school.

His role, he had made sure to establish, was a fluid one. He had gone from protestor in situ to keen observer of human nature and general do-gooder who cared about the environment. He'd been vague about his actual background but had somehow managed to imply that he was more than just a drifter out to attach himself to a worthwhile cause. He'd used his imagination and he knew that a lot of the protestors were beginning to turn to him to answer some of their questions.

It irked him that even as he tried to find a solution to the situation and even as he mentally worked out the cost of digging into his pocket to effectively buy them off when there was, technically, no need for him to do so, he was still managing to feel bloody guilty at his charade.

He'd had no idea his conscience was so hyperactive and it got on his nerves.

Although…he had to admit a certain desire to impress the woman he was sharing a house with—fistfuls of cash would mean she could do the improvements she needed. He was cynical enough to suspect that if sufficient hard cash was put on the table she would not be able to resist because she was human and humans were all, without exception, susceptible to the lure of money.

Trouble was, he had to content himself with the painting job she had delegated to him.

'You don't have to,' she had said two days previously, when she had led him to a part of the house that looked as though the cobwebs had set up camp the day after the final brick in the house had been laid. 'You pay rent and, believe me, that's sufficient help.'

But Art had felt obliged to make good on his vague assurances that he was capable of helping out.

Besides, painting the room was proving to be a valuable way of avoiding her because the more contact he had with her, the more interested he became in digging deeper, past the polite conversation they shared, usually in the company of a million other people. After that first night she had shared nothing more about herself. They had had no time alone together. Her house was apparently a magnet for every person in the village who had nothing better to do than drop by for a chat.

The night before, someone she had bumped into several weeks previously had shown up for an informal chat about a problem he was having with his new employer, who had taken over the company and was trying to get rid of all the old retainers by fair means or foul.

To Art's amazement, Rose had been happy to feed the guy and give him free advice. Little wonder she didn't have much money going spare when she failed to charge for most of her services.

Her absolute lack of interest in making money should have been anathema to him but the opposite appeared to be the case. The more she invited the world into her house, the more he wanted her to slam the front door so that he could have her all to himself.

Nothing to do with the reason he was here.

Just because…he wanted to have her all to himself.

He'd managed to find a couple of hours during which he'd touched base with several of his clients and answered a couple of urgent emails and then he'd done some painting.

Now, at a little after six-thirty, he stood back to inspect his efforts and was quietly pleased with what he had managed. The mucus shade of green was slowly being replaced by something off-white and bland. Big improvement.

Still in paint-spattered clothes, Art went downstairs, fully expecting to find a few more waifs and strays in the kitchen, but instead there was just Rose sitting at the kitchen table, poring over a file.

From the doorway, he stood and looked, giving in to the steady pulse of desire rippling through him like a forbidden drumbeat. She was frowning, her slender hands cupping her face as she peered down at the stack of papers in front of her. She reached to absently remove the clasp from her hair and he sucked in a sharp breath as it fell around her shoulders in a tumble of uncontrolled curls. Deep chestnut brown…shades of dark auburn…paler strands of toffee…a riot of vibrant colour that took his breath away.

For once she wasn't wearing something long and shapeless but instead a pair of faded blue jeans and an old grey cropped tee shirt and, from the way she was hunched over the table, he was afforded a tantalising glimpse of her cleavage.

She looked up, caught his eye and sat back.

She stretched and half yawned and the forbidden drumbeat surged into a tidal wave of primal desire.

No bra.

He could see the jut of her nipples against the soft

cotton and the caution he had been meticulously cul-
tivating over the past few days disappeared in a puff
of smoke.

His erection was as solid as a shaft of steel and he
had to look away to gather himself for a few vital seconds or else risk losing the plot altogether.

'Took the afternoon off.' Rose smiled and stood up.
'Hence the casual gear. Drink? Tea? Coffee? Something
stronger? I've actually gone out and bought some wine.'

'The rent I pay doesn't cover food. It's Friday. Allow
me to take you out for a meal.'

Rose hesitated. She hadn't been out for a meal with a
man for ages. She was twenty-eight years old and the
thrills of her social life could be written on the back of
a postage stamp.

'Restaurants will be packed out.' She laughed, anticipation bubbling up inside her. 'Tourists…'

'We can venture further afield. Name the place and
I'll reserve a table.'

'Don't be silly. You don't have to…'

'You don't have to…?' Arturo shot her a wry look
from under sooty lashes. 'Anyone who knows me at all
would know that those four words would never apply to
me because I make it my duty never to feel that I have to
do anything I don't want to do. If I didn't want to take
you out to dinner I would never have issued the invitation in the first place. Now, name the place.'

God, Rose thought, who would ever think that she
would go for a guy who took charge? She was much
more into the sensitive kind of guy who consulted and

discussed. Arturo Frank couldn't have been less of a consulting and discussing man, and yet a pleasurable shiver rippled through her as she met his deep, dark eyes. 'Name the place? Now, let me think about that. How generous are you feeling tonight…?'

Rose shocked herself because she wasn't flirtatious by nature. Her mother had always been the flirt, which was probably why she had ended up where she had. That was a characteristic Rose had made sure to squash, not that there had ever been any evidence of it being there in the first place.

But she felt like a flirt as their eyes tangled and she half smiled with her head tilted pensively to one side.

'I'm just kidding.' She grinned and ran her fingers through her tangled hair. 'There are a couple of excellent pizza places in the next village along. I can call and reserve a table. So…in answer to your invitation, it's a yes.'

'I'm saying no to the cheap and cheerful pizza place,' Arturo delivered with a dismissive gesture, eyes still glued to her face.

'In that case…'

'Leave it with me. I'll sort it.'

'You will?'

'Expect something slightly more upmarket than a fast-food joint.'

'In which case, I'll naturally share the bill.'

'That won't be happening. When I ask a woman out, she doesn't go near her wallet.'

There she went, tingling all over again! Behaving like the frothy, frilly, girly girl she had never been. He was so macho, so alpha male, so incredibly intelligent, and yet he cared about all the things she cared about. She prided herself on being savvy but she could feel the ground slip beneath her feet and she liked the way it felt, enjoyed the heady sensation of falling.

She wasn't interested in any man who was just passing through, but a little voice asked inside her head... *What if she took a risk?* After all, where had being careful got her?

And an even more treacherous little voice whispered seductively, *What if he delays his plans to move on...? In the end all nomads found their resting ground, didn't they? And there were jobs aplenty for a guy as smart and proactive as he was...*

'Okay.'

'You look a little bemused. What kind of guys have you gone out with in the past? Did they take out their calculator at the end of the meal so that they could split the bill in half? Call me antiquated—' his voice lowered to a murmur '—but I enjoy being generous with the women I take out.'

So we're going on a date.

Excitement surged through Rose in a disturbing, all-consuming tidal wave.

Maybe—she brought herself back down to earth—it wasn't a date. As such. Maybe it was simply his way of saying thank you for renting a room in her house and having whatever food and drink he wanted at his disposal. He was paying her a lot more than she'd wanted but it was still a lot less than if he'd been staying in even the cheapest of the local hotels.

But the warmth of his gaze was still turning her head

to mush when, an hour later and with no idea where they would be going, she stood in front of her wardrobe surveying the uninspiring collection of comfortable clothes that comprised her going-out gear.

It bore witness to the alarming fact that when it came to going out she had become decidedly lazy over time. Easy evenings with friends, the occasional movie, casual suppers at the kitchen table, for which she could have shown up in her PJs and no one would really have cared one way or the other.

In fact, working largely from the house as she did, her work clothes were interchangeable with her casual wear. Everything blurred into loose-fitting and shapeless.

Practical, she reminded herself, hand brushing past the baggy culottes to linger on the one and only figure-hugging skirt she possessed. Her wardrobe was filled with practical clothes because she was, above all else, practical. Her mother had had the monopoly on impulsive behaviour. She, Rose, was practical.

Yet she didn't feel practical as she wriggled into the clinging jade-green skirt and the only slightly less clinging black top with the little pearl buttons down the front, the top four of which she undid. Then promptly did back up.

There was little she could do with her hair, but she liked the way it hung in a riot of curls over her shoulders, and when she plunged her feet into her one and only pair of high-heeled shoes…well, she would have dwarfed a lot of men but she wasn't going to dwarf the one who would be waiting for her downstairs.

In fact, she would be elevated to his level. Eye to eye...nose to nose...*mouth to mouth...*

Waiting for her in the kitchen with a glass of wine in his hand, Art was just off the phone from one of the finest restaurants in the area. He wasn't sure how he was going to explain away the extravagance but he was sick of mealtimes being pot luck, along the lines of a bring-and-buy sale in someone's backyard.

He was also sick of conversations with her being halted by someone popping their head around the door. She worked from her house and so seemed accessible to any and everyone. While he had been busy planting questions in the heads of all those protestors squatting on his land in the misguided belief that they were going to halt the march of progress, he hadn't actually got around to planting a single question in Rose's head because he never seemed to find the time to be alone with her for longer than five seconds.

He was also disgruntled and frustrated at the tantalising glimpses of her personal life which he had been unable to explore. He accepted that that was just thwarted curiosity but it was still frustrating. He existed on a diet of being able to get exactly what he wanted, and that included a woman's full and undivided attention.

She had told him something about herself and he had found himself wanting to hear more and had been unable to. When had that ever happened before? Given half a chance, there was no woman he could think of who wouldn't have clawed her way back to that interrupted personal conversation with the tenacity of a tigress.

But no. It was almost as though Rose had more pressing things to do than talk to him.

And yet...there was *something* between them. He felt it and so did she. It was just not big enough for her to actually put herself out to try to cultivate it and that irked him.

All in all, he was looking forward to this meal out more than he could remember looking forward to anything in a long time.

He swirled the wine in his glass, looked down at the golden liquid and then, when he looked up...

There she was.

Art straightened. His mouth fell open. Rooted to the spot, he could feel the throb of sexual awareness flower and bloom into something hot and urgent and pressing.

She was...bloody *stunning*.

That body, long-limbed and rangy under the challenging attire, was spectacular. Lean and toned and effortlessly graceful. She lacked the practised art of the catwalk model, the strutting posture and the moody expression, and she was all the sexier for that.

And she wasn't wearing a bra.

He did his utmost not to stare at the small, rounded pertness of her breasts and the indentation of pebbly nipples pushing against the fine cotton.

He could see Rose's whole body react to that leisurely appraisal and the horrified look on her face which accompanied her involuntary response. It galvanised her into speech and action at the same time, moving into the kitchen whilst simultaneously pinning a bright smile to her face as she quizzed him on where they were going.

Art snapped out of his trance.

'I'll just grab my bag.' She interrupted her nervous chatter to look around her.

'Why?'

'Car keys, for one thing!' she announced gaily.

The kitchen felt too small for both of them to be in it. He was wearing nothing more than a pair of dark trousers and a white shirt, staple components of any wardrobe, and yet he looked jaw-droppingly beautiful. He filled the contours of the shirt to perfection. She could see the ripple of muscle under the fabric and he had rolled the sleeves up so that her eyes were drawn to his forearms, liberally sprinkled with dark, silky hair. The minute her eyes went there they couldn't help but move further along to his long brown fingers and it was then a hop and a skip until she wondered what those fingers would feel like…on her and…*in her.*

'What? Sorry?'

Had he said something?

'I've ordered a taxi so there's no need for you to drive,' he delivered smoothly, allowing her no time to lodge a protest.

'You're so good at taking over,' Rose murmured, blushing and smiling.

'I can't help it,' Arturo said without apology. 'It's part of my personality.'

He lowered his eyes and offered his arm to her.

'It's been a while since…'

'Since?'

'Since I've been out for a meal.'

'You mean…on a date?'

'Is that what this is?' They were outside and he was opening the car door for her, waiting as she slid into the back seat before joining her. 'I thought…' she turned to him and breathed in the clean, woody smell of him, which made her want to pass out '…that this was just your way of thanking me for putting you up. Not—' she laughed '—that it's been any bother at all!'

'That as well…'

'You needn't have.'

'Again. Those annoying words. It's not a declaration of intent,' he interjected, then his voice lowered. 'It's a… I haven't told you, but you look…remarkable…'

'I know it's not a declaration of intent! You're just passing through and, besides, you're the guy who doesn't do domesticity, home cooking or women asking personal questions. And thank you for the compliment, by the way. I… I haven't worn this old outfit in a long time.'

Her breathing was jerky and she took refuge in gazing through the window at the familiar countryside. She had no idea where they were going, but it wasn't long before she found out because she recognised the impressive drive that led to one of the top hotels in the county, where a famous Michelin-starred chef produced food she could never have afforded in a million years.

She turned to him, her face a picture of bemusement and shock.

'I recently came into some money,' Arturo said smoothly, 'and I can't think of a better way of spending some of it than on bringing you here.'

'I'm not dressed for this place.'

'Do you care what other people think?' He swung out of the car and walked around to open her door.

'Who doesn't?'

'I don't.'

'Maybe it's a legacy from when my mum went away.' Rose was agog as they were shown into the splendid hotel and then escorted like royalty to the most impressive dining room she had ever been in. She was hardly aware of what she was saying. She was way too focused on trying to take in everything around her.

'You were saying…?' he said as soon as they were seated, a corner table with a bird's eye view of the richly ornate interior.

'I was saying that my eyes are popping out.' She swivelled to look at him and her breathing became shallow. What money, she wondered, had he come into? But then, hot on the heels of that thought, came another—her mother had been the recipient of an equally surprising inheritance. Stranger things happened in life. It certainly explained how he was footloose and fancy free…and able to indulge his interest in saving the countryside.

And if he was generous by nature, as he clearly was, then he would probably travel around until the cash ran out before returning to whatever job he had had before. That was a small detail he had never filled her in on.

He'd warned her off reading anything into this dinner invitation but he was crazy if he thought that she wasn't going to be impressed to death by his generosity and by the time and effort he'd put into sourcing this place for them. God only knew how he'd managed to wangle a table but she had seen, in his interactions with the people on the site, that he could charm the birds from the trees.

'And you were telling me why it is that you care about what people think...'

Rose looked at him. He'd shaved but still managed to look darkly dangerous. There was a stillness about him that made her nerves race and brought a fine prickle of perspiration to her skin. Something about the lazy intensity of his eyes when they focused on her.

'And how long did your mother go away for?'

'Two years,' Rose admitted, flattered at his interest.

'Two *years*?'

'I know in the big scheme of things it doesn't seem like a lifetime but, believe me, when you're a kid and you're waiting by the window it *feels* never-ending.'

'In the big scheme of things it bloody *is* never-ending, Rose, and to a kid... How old *were* you?'

'Eight.'

'Eight.' Art was shocked. His father had lost the plot for very similar reasons, which pretty much said everything there was to say on the subject of love, but abandonment had not been an issue. 'Where did you stay... at the age of eight...while your mother vanished on her soul-seeking mission?'

'You shouldn't be too hard on her. She was screwed up at the time. I stayed in the village, of course. Where else? I lived with the neighbours. I'm not sure whether they thought that they'd be hanging onto me for as long as they had to but they were wonderful. That said, I knew there was gossip and that hurt. I was saved from a much harsher fate when my mother started acting up because I happened to live where I did. In a small village that protected its own. I owe them.'

'You owe them…the entire village…a sizeable debt. So…' this half to himself '…*that's* why this fight is so personal to you.'

'Something like that. But you must be bored stiff listening to me rattle on.'

'The opposite.' Art forced himself to relax. All problems had solutions and he was solution-orientated. 'I've wandered through the village,' he said, adroitly changing the subject as he perused the menu without looking at her. 'I'm surprised you haven't thought to use a little bribery and blackmail with the developers who want the land you're occupying…'

'Sorry?' Rose's head shot up and she stared at him with a frown.

'You recall I asked Phil to have a look at the paperwork? Not because I'm any kind of expert, but I wanted to see for myself what the legal position was with the land. Some of the protesters out there have been asking questions…'

'You never mentioned that to me.'

'Should I have? Passing interest. Nothing more.' Art paused. 'The land is sold and there's nothing anyone can do about that.'

'You'd be surprised how public opinion can alter the outcome of something unpleasant.' Rose's lips firmed. She wasn't sure whether to fume at his intrusion or be pleased at his intelligent interest in the situation.

'People might be open to alternative lines of approach,' he implied, shutting his menu and sitting back.

'You're very optimistic if you think that a company the size of DC Logistics would be interested in anything other than steamrollering over us. We're fighting fire with fire and if we lose...then we can make sure that life isn't easy for them as they go ahead with their conscienceless development.'

'Or you could try another tack. Apparently the local school could do with a lot of refurbishment. The sports ground is in dire need of repair. One section of the building that was damaged by fire last year is still out of bounds. Frankly, that's a lawsuit waiting to happen. Ever thought that instead of threatening a company that has deeds to the land, you could always coerce them into doing their bit for the community?'

'You've certainly been digging deep.' Rose sat back and looked at Art. 'Have you been discussing this alternative with my protestors?'

'They're not *your* protestors,' he fielded coolly, meeting her gaze without blinking. 'If you have deeper, more personal reasons for your fight, then they don't necessarily share those reasons. They might be open to other ways of dealing with the situation.'

Wine was being brought to the table. He waited until the waiter had poured them both a glass then he raised his.

'But enough of this. We're not here to talk about the land, are we? That said...it's just something you might want to think about.'

CHAPTER FIVE

IT WAS THE best meal she had ever had in her life although, as she reluctantly left a morsel of the *crème brulée* in its dish because she physically couldn't manage another mouthful, Rose had to admit that it was much more than the quality of the food that had made the evening quite perfect.

It was the fact that she was here with Arturo.

They had not had an opportunity to talk, to really talk, since he had moved in and for four hours they more than made up for that. He was fascinating. He knew *so much*. He could converse with ease on any topic and he had a wonderful knack of drawing her out of herself, making her open up in a way that revealed to her just how private she had become over the years.

He could be self-deprecating one minute and, almost without pausing to draw breath, ruin the illusion by being astoundingly arrogant—but arrogant in a way that somehow didn't manage to get on her nerves. She couldn't understand how that was in any way, shape or form possible...but it clearly was.

And he'd made her think—about the protest and

other ways that might be found to bring about a positive outcome. He had touched only once more on the subject and the notion of inevitability had been aired—yes, it was inevitable that the land would be developed, but that suggestion he had planted in her head was beginning to look quite promising. She had certain trump cards and there was much that could be done to improve the village.

She was tipsy and happy as they stepped out into the velvety black night.

'I haven't had such a lovely time in ages,' she confided as a taxi pulled to a stop as soon as they were outside. She waited until he was in the back seat with her before turning to him. The darkness turned his face into a mosaic of hard shadows and angles and, just for a few seconds, she felt a tingle of apprehension that warred with the warm, melting feeling making her limbs heavy and pleasantly blurring her thoughts.

She was smiling—grinning like a Cheshire cat—but he was quite serious as he looked at her.

'You look as though you can't wait for the evening to end,' she said lightly, sobering up, smile wavering. 'Don't blame you. You must be accustomed to far more exciting company than me.'

Looking back at her, Art thought that she couldn't have been further from the truth. He hadn't sat and talked with any woman for that length of time for years. In the normal course of events, an expensive meal would have included some light conversation but the evening would have been overlaid with the assumption of sex and the conversation would have been geared towards that.

'What makes you say that?'

'Something about you,' Rose admitted truthfully. 'You're not like anyone I've ever met before and if I can see that, then so can everyone else. You strike me as the sort of guy who's never short of female company. Is that why you steer clear of involvement? Because you don't see the point of settling down when there are so many fish in the sea?'

'I steer clear of involvement because I watched my father ruined by too much of it.'

'Oh.' Rose paused. 'How so?' she asked seriously.

Art had surprised himself by that admission and now he wondered what to say. A series of divorces? A carousel of avaricious blonde bombshells who had been out to feather their own nests? A fortune depleted by the demands of alimony payments? Where to start?

Art had been defined by one disillusionment after another, from the isolation he had had to endure as a child when his father had retreated into himself after his wife's sudden death to the abruptness of having to deal with boarding school, and all played out to the steady drumbeat of his father's failed relationships and the consequent, expensive fallout.

He shifted, stared briefly out of the window then back at her. Her gaze was calm, interested but without fuss and fanfare—curious but not overly so.

'My father had a habit of repeating his mistakes,' Art told her heavily. 'He was always quick to get involved, only to regret his involvement but then, just when he'd managed to free himself from one woman, he would repeat the cycle all over again. Your mother had her way of coping with losing her husband…' His mouth twisted into a crooked smile. 'My father coped in a slightly different way.'

'But in a way that would have equally damaging consequences… We certainly didn't strike jackpot when it came to childhood experiences, did we?' She shot him a rueful smile and reached out, almost impulsively, to rest her hand on his.

The warmth of her hand zapped through him like a powerful electric charge, tightening his groin and sending a heavy, pounding ache between his thighs.

With relief, he recognised that the taxi was pulling up outside her house.

He was in urgent need of a cold shower. Maybe even a cold bath. Blocks of ice would have to play a part. Anything to cool the onset of his ardour.

'All experience,' he said neutrally, pushing open his door and glancing back at her over his shoulder in a gesture that implied an end to the conversation, 'is good experience, in my opinion. But I'm very glad you enjoyed the evening.'

He all but sprinted to the front door. She fumbled with the front door key and he relieved her of it, acutely aware of the brush of her skin against his.

'I don't usually drink as much as I did tonight,' Rose apologised with a little breathy laugh, stepping past him into the hall. 'I'm beginning to think that I should get out more, live a little…'

'All work and no play… You know the saying…'

* * *

For a few moments they both stood in the semi-dark-
ened hallway, staring at one another in taut silence,
and the breath caught in her throat because she could
see the lick of desire in his eyes, a sexual speculation
that set her ablaze with frantic desire because it mirrored her own.

'Right, well...' Rose was the first to break the lengthening silence. 'Thanks again for a brilliant evening...'
She began turning away but then felt his hand circle
her arm and she stilled, heart racing, pulse racing—
everything racing.

'Rose...'

With one foot planted firmly in the comfort zone of
common sense and the other dangling precariously and
recklessly over the edge of a precipice, Rose looked at
him, holding herself rigid with tension.

'It would be madness.' Arturo looked away, looked
back to her, looked away again, restless and uncomfortable in his own skin and yet powerless to relieve
either discomfort.

'What?' Rose whispered.

'You know what. This. Us. Taking this any further.'

For a few seconds she didn't say anything, then eventually she murmured, briefly breaking their electrifying eye contact, 'I agree.'

'You can't even begin to understand the complications...'

'Do I need to?'

'Explain.'

'We're not anticipating a relationship.' She tilted her

chin at a defiant angle. Sex for the sake of sex? She'd never contemplated that. The urgent demands of lust, the taste of a passion that was powerful enough to make a nonsense of her principles...well, those were things that had never blotted her horizon. 'We don't have to think about all the complications or all the reasons why it wouldn't make sense for us to...to...' She reddened and caught his eye.

'Make wild, passionate love until we just can't any longer?'

'You're just passing through...'

'Sure that doesn't bother you? Because I won't be staying. A week, tops, and I'll be gone and that'll be the last you'll ever see of me.'

'You wouldn't be curious to see where the protest you joined will end up?'

'I know where it'll end up.' He clearly didn't want to talk about that. He raised his arm to stroke her cheek with the back of his hand, a light, feathery touch that made her sigh and close her eyes.

'Let's go upstairs,' she breathed unevenly, her eyes fluttering open to gaze at his impossibly handsome face. She stepped back and took his hand. If this was wrong, then why did it feel so *right*? Before hitting the stairs, she kicked her shoes off and then padded up ahead of him, still holding his hand, glancing back over her shoulder twice, wishing that she knew what was going through his head.

She shyly pushed open her bedroom door and stepped in, ignoring the overhead light in favour of the lamp by her bed, which cast an immediate mellow glow through the room.

It was a large square room, with high ceilings and both picture rails and dado rails.

Arturo had not been in it before. He looked around briefly and then grinned. 'I didn't take you for having such a sense of drama…'

Rose laughed, walked towards him and linked her arms around his waist. 'I'm sensible when it comes to pretty much everything but—' she looked at the dreamy four-poster king-sized bed with floaty curtains and dark, soft-as-silk bed linen '—I used to dream of having a four-poster bed when I was a kid.'

'Was that when you were waiting for your mother to reappear?' Art murmured, burying his face into her hair and breathing in the sweet smell of the floral shampoo she used.

'How did you guess?'

'I'm tuned in like that.' A memory came from nowhere to knock him for six—a memory of his mother leaning over him, smiling, with a book in one hand. Had she just read him a story? Was she about to? She was dressed up, going out for the evening.

He clenched his jaw as the vivid image faded. 'Enough talk,' he growled, edging them both towards the bed. Rose giggled as her knees hit the mattress and she toppled backwards, taking him with her, although he niftily deflected the bulk of his weight from landing directly on her. But he remained where he was, flat on his back next to her.

'The canopy has stars,' he commented, amused, and he heard the grin in her voice when she replied.

'That's the hidden romantic in me.'

Art turned his head to look at her and she did likewise.

'You don't have to worry,' she said flatly, before he could jump in with another warning lecture on his nomadic tendencies—warning her off the temptation to look for more involvement than was on the table.

'Worry about what?'

'I may have the occasional romantic lapse, but I'm pretty level-headed when it comes to men, and latching onto a good-looking guy who has an aversion to putting down roots is the last sort of guy who would tick any boxes for me.'

'I tick at least *one* box,' Art murmured, smiling very slowly.

'Well, yes…you tick that one box.' Flustered, she held her breath as their eyes locked.

'Never knock the physical attraction box. It's the biggest one of all.'

'We'll have to agree to differ on that.'

'Think so?' Art grinned, settling on his side and manoeuvring her so that they were now facing one another, clothes still on and that very fact sending the temperature into the sizzling stratosphere. 'Oh, I wouldn't talk too fast if I were you…' He slipped his hand under her top and took his time getting to her breast, waiting until her breathing had become halting, her eyelids fluttering and her nostrils flaring. Then and only then did he touch her, cup her naked breast, feel the tight bud of her nipple. He'd spent the meal in a state of heightened awareness and the feel of her now was electrifying.

While he was busy telling her just how fast he could make her believe in the importance of sexual attraction because nothing was better than good sex, and he was very, *very* adept at giving very, *very* good sex, he was simultaneously on the verge of blowing it by getting turned on too quickly. In his book, speed and good sex rarely went together for a sensational experience.

He kept looking at her, holding her gaze, while he played with her nipple.

He wasn't going to go a step further until he got himself under control.

But, hell, those sexy eyes that were just on the right side of innocent, however sassy she was, were doing a million things to his body.

'You think you can convert me?' Rose breathed, squirming with want.

'No harm in trying.' Art let loose a low, sexy laugh. In one slick movement, he eased himself up to straddle her prone body, caging her in with his thighs. He hooked his fingers under the top and began slowly tugging it up.

'No bra,' he murmured. 'I like that.'

'I...' Rose gulped and wished that she hadn't switched any lights on at all, although would she have sacrificed the joy of looking at him to preserve her modesty? She felt faint as her top rode higher and then the whisper of cool air brought goosebumps to her naked skin. Automatically, she lifted her arms to cross them over her bare chest and, just as fast, Arturo gently pushed them aside and stifled a primal groan of pleasure as his eyes feasted on her.

'Beautiful,' he whispered, circling one straining bud with the tip of his finger.

Rose had never felt quite so exposed. She wasn't ashamed of her body. She simply recognised its limitations. Lights off worked when it came to dealing with those limitations and to have him looking at her like that...

She sneaked a glance at him and felt a surge of thrilling excitement because his eyes were dark with masculine appreciation.

'I'm not exactly the most voluptuous woman on the face of the earth,' Rose apologised, blushing. 'That's why I can go without a bra a lot of the time. Not much there to contain.' She laughed and watched his finger as it continued to circle her nipple, moving onto the other.

'You should never have hang-ups about your body,' Arturo said thickly. 'It's amazing. Your nipples are stunning...dark...*succulent*...'

'Arturo!'

He laughed and shot her a wicked look from under his lashes. 'Is that the sound of you begging me to continue telling you why you should be proud of your body?'

'No!' But she laughed, a little breathless laugh that was unsteady with anticipation.

'I'm going to have fun tasting them,' Arturo told her conversationally. 'Does it turn you on to imagine the feel of my mouth on your nipple?'

'Stop!'

'You're red as a beetroot.' Arturo grinned and gently tilted her averted face so that she was looking at him.

He vaulted off the bed, fumbled to make sure protection was handy and then he began getting undressed.

Rose stared.

She forgot all about her inhibitions because never had she seen anything so glorious in her life before.

He was all muscle and sinew, his broad shoulders tapering to a washboard-flat stomach. He ditched the shirt and raised his eyebrows with amusement at her rapt expression.

'You have no idea,' he murmured, taking a step towards her, at which she promptly hoisted herself onto her elbows, automatically leaning towards him, 'what that expression is doing to my libido.'

'Really?' Riveted, Rose continued to stare at him.

'Really,' Arturo said drily, 'but you'll see for yourself soon enough...' He burst out laughing when her eyes skittered away just as he began unbuttoning his trousers.

He seemed to revel in the intensity of her gaze.

The trousers were off.

The boxers followed suit.

Rose gulped. He was more than impressive. Big, thick, throbbing with *want*. Standing there, he was absolutely lacking in inhibition, carelessly indifferent to the perfection of his nakedness.

Rose sat up, then slid off the bed to stand in front of him. She was half naked and now all she wanted to do was yank down the skirt but, before she could, he stayed her fluttering hand and moved towards her, holding her just for a moment so that she could feel his hardness pressing against her belly.

'Allow me...' he murmured.

Arturo wasn't going to rush anything, even though his body must be clamouring for satisfaction.

He eased the skin-tight skirt off her to reveal plain cotton panties. For a few seconds, Arturo stilled.

He was kneeling and he drew back to look at her. Hands on her bare bottom, Arturo delicately teased the folds of her womanhood with a gentle touch, causing her to gasp and then exhale on a whimper.

When his tongue slid into the slippery crease she gasped again, this time on a guttural moan, and her fingers curled into his hair as she opened her legs wider to receive his attentions.

Rose was melting. Every bone in her body was turning to water as his tongue flicked over her, squirming deeper until he located the pulsing bud of her core.

The pleasure was intense, unbearable almost, nothing that she had ever felt before or could ever have imagined feeling. It was pure sensation and every thought, confused or otherwise, shot straight out of her head.

She realised that she was moving against his mouth in an unconscious rhythm.

She almost squeaked a protest when he drew back and stood up to lift her off her feet so that he could deposit her onto the bed, as though she weighed nothing at all.

Rose was expecting something fast and furious but instead he pinned her hands above her head, ordered her not to move a muscle and then sat back on his haunches to gaze at her with open admiration.

If this was how he was in bed with a woman, she thought in a heated daze, then she was surprised that there wasn't a demanding queue of ex-lovers banging on her front door, braying for him to return to bed with them.

'Just for the moment,' he said huskily, 'indulge me and allow me to take charge.'

With her hands still above her head, burrowed underneath the pillow, Rose half smiled.

'Are you trying to tell me that you don't take charge in everything you do?' she teased, 'because if you are then I don't believe you.'

'It's true. Some people have accused me of occasionally being somewhat…assertive.'

He seemed determined to assert himself right now. Starting with her breasts.

He kissed them, nuzzled their softness, making her writhe and stretch underneath him, her movements feline and sensuous. He licked one nipple with his tongue and then sucked on it, drawing it into his mouth and teasing the sensitive tip with his tongue. As he ministered to her breast, he dipped down to rest his hand between her thighs, lightly covering her mound with the palm of his hand and then pressing down in lazy circular movements.

Bliss.

Rose was dripping wet and she didn't care. She was explosively turned on. Something about the position of her arms heightened the sensitivity of her breasts and each flick of his tongue and caress of his hand made her want to cry out loud.

He trailed a path of kisses along her stomach and she inhaled sharply, wanting more than anything for him to taste her *down there* again, there between her legs where the ache desperately craved his touch.

As he found that place and began, once again, to tease her with his tongue, she arched up, spread her legs wider and bucked against his questing mouth.

Sensation started with an electric ripple that spread outwards with the force of a tsunami until she was lost in a world dictated by her physical response to his mouth. She could no more have strung a coherent thought together than she could have grown wings and taken flight.

When she came against his mouth it was with such force that she cried out, hands clutching the bed linen, her whole body arching, stiffening and then shuddering as everything exploded inside her.

She eventually subsided on a wave of mind-blowing contentment.

'Felt good?' Arturo lay alongside her, then curved her against him, pushing his thigh between her legs.

Rose linked her fingers around his neck and darted some kisses over his face. 'I'm sorry.' She looked at him with such genuine apology that he winced.

'Sorry about what?'

'Just lying there and…um…enjoying myself…'

'You have no idea how much enjoyment I got from pleasuring you.'

Rose smiled and curved against him, taking the initiative this time, adoring the hard, muscled lines of his body as she ran her hands over it. Along his shoulders, over his hard, sinewy chest, taking time to tease his flattened brown nipples.

His erection was thick and pulsing and she lowered herself into a position where she could take him into her mouth and he, manoeuvring her, could take her into his.

An exchange of intense pleasure that brought her right back up to the edge from which she had only recently descended.

Rose had never experienced such a lack of inhibition. She had always approached the opposite sex from a position of caution, a place where mechanisms were in place to prevent her from being too hurt. She'd never let go with anyone, not that her life had been cluttered with an abundance of men, and it astounded her that, of all the people in the world, she should be so free and open with one who wasn't destined to play any kind of permanent role in her life.

It didn't make sense.

But wonderfully open was exactly what she was feeling as she licked and teased and sucked him, as she felt him move between her thighs, tickling her with his tongue, their bodies fused as one.

They both knew when the time was right for the foreplay to end before it cascaded into orgasm.

Arturo eased her off him, groaning as their bodies broke contact. It was a matter of a few fumbling seconds and then, protection in place, he positioned himself over her.

Rose could barely contain her excitement. Her whole

body ached for the ultimate satisfaction of having him inside her and when he drove into her, thrusting hard and firm, she groaned long and low.

He filled her up and with each thrust she came closer and closer to the brink.

Art had never been with anyone as responsive as she was. It was as though he was tuned in to her, sensitive to just how far he could take her before she came, able to time his own orgasm to match hers, and when they came it was mind-blowing.

Deep inside her, embedded to the hilt, he drove hard and felt her shudder and cry out just as he rocked with waves of such intense pleasure that he couldn't contain his own guttural cry of satisfaction.

It was a few moments before they could unglue their bodies from one another. Unusually, Art didn't immediately feel the urge to break the connection by escaping to have a shower.

Instead, he slid off her and held her. What the hell had he done? He'd come here on a mission and this most definitely had *not* been any part of his mission.

But he looked down at her flushed face, her parted mouth, felt the warmth of her beautiful body pressed against his, and all he wanted to do was have her all over again.

Art knew that this was a weakness. In fact, sleeping with her at all had been a weakness. Since when had *any* woman taken precedence over common sense and, more importantly, work?

And what happened now?

Art knew what *should* happen. He should walk away. He should walk away and keep on walking until he hit London and the reality of his life there. He should put an immediate end to this charade and conduct whatever business needed conducting through his lawyers and accountants. The land belonged to him and tiptoeing around that stark fact was a matter of choice rather than necessity.

Okay, so maybe if she got stuck in and took a stand, the community would view his development as a blot on their landscape and react accordingly to the newcomers buying properties, but that wouldn't last. Within six months everything would settle down and life would carry on as normal.

His presence here and his willingness to do his best to ease the process would bear testimony to his capacity for goodwill.

It would also be useful because, in due course, he would be putting in another planning application and a hostile community would make that more difficult.

But in the end he would get what he wanted because he always did.

And, in the meantime, this...was a complication.

'What are you thinking?' Rose asked drowsily, opening her eyes to look directly at him. 'No,' she continued, 'I know what you're thinking.'

'Mind reader, are you?' Art smiled and kissed the tip of her nose. He cupped her naked breast with his hand and marvelled at how nicely it fitted. Not too big, not too small.

'You're thinking that it's time you went back to your

bedroom and you'd be right because it's late and I want to go to sleep.'

'Is that the sound of you kicking me out of your bedroom?' he murmured, moving in to nibble her ear and then licking the side of her neck so that she squirmed and giggled softly.

'It's the sound of a woman who needs her beauty sleep.' She wriggled away from him so that she could head for the bathroom.

'But what,' Art heard himself ask, 'does a red-blooded man do if he wakes in the early hours of the morning and needs his woman by his side?'

Rose stilled but when she answered her voice was still light and teasing. 'He goes downstairs for a glass of milk?'

'Wrong answer.' Art heaved himself into a sitting position and pulled her towards him. 'I never thought I'd hear myself say this, but let's spend the night together...and, by the way... I'd like it if you called me Art. Not Arthur...not Arturo. Art.'

CHAPTER SIX

ART GAZED AT the vast swathes of empty land around him. Open fields. The very same open fields that had confronted him on day one when he had arrived with a plan and a deadline.

Slight difference now. The plan and the deadline had both taken a battering. He'd slept with Rose over a week and a half ago and even as his head had urged him to turn his back and walk away, his body had argued against that course of action and had won.

They'd shared a bed every night since then. He couldn't see her without wanting her. It was insane but whatever attraction kept pulling him towards her, it was bigger than all the reserves of willpower at his disposal.

And the land...

Art strolled to the very spot where the protesters had set up camp. There were some stragglers but most had left. He'd been busy arguing his corner whilst making sure not to stand on any soapboxes bellowing his opinions. He'd listened to everything that had been said and had quickly sussed that, however fervent they were about the abstract notion of the land being developed, when it came down to basics, the offer of those very same heartless developers doing some good for their community had won the day.

Financial assistance for the primary school; a fund towards the local library, which also served as a meeting place for most of the senior citizens; playing fields to be included on some of his land which, as it happened, suited Art very well indeed, bearing in mind his future plans for the site.

Art had advised them to contact the team of lawyers working for DC Logistics.

'There's always a solution when it comes to sorting problems,' he had asserted, safe in the knowledge that they would find no hindrance to their requests. Not only was he happy to ease the situation but he was positively pleased to be able to do so because he had grown fond of all of them, had seen for himself, first-hand, how strongly they felt about the land.

In London, community spirit of that kind was noticeably absent and he'd been impressed by what he'd seen.

And, crucially, Rose had more or less conceded that it was the best solution because, like it or not, those tractors and cranes would move in sooner or later.

His job here was done and satisfactorily so.

He could be pleased with himself. He could start thinking about step two. He knew in his gut that there would be no obstacles in his way and step two had always been top of the agenda. Art might have been cynical when it came to the romantic notion of love, but familial love, discovered in the most unexpected of places, had settled in his heart and filled the space there.

He'd thought outside the box and it had paid off. Now, as he looked at his land, he realised that thinking outside the box and getting what he'd wanted had come at an unexpected cost.

Rose.

He abruptly turned away, headed for the battered Land Rover which couldn't have been more different from his own fleet of super-charged, high-performance cars.

She'd temporarily loaned him her car.

'I'll be buried in case files for the next week or so.' She had laughed, her arms wound around his neck, her eyes sparkling, her half-clad body pressed against his. 'You'll want to be out and about. Lord knows you've become some kind of mentor to half the protesters...with that promise of yours that the developers are going to meet their extravagant demands! Mind you, I'll be pleased to have my kitchen table back.'

Art would have to come clean. There was no way around it. He couldn't believe that he had been disingenuous enough, when thoughts had entered his head about sleeping with her, to believe that he could have a fling and walk away.

Two adults, he had argued to himself. Two consenting adults who fancied one another. What was the problem? All he had to do was make it clear to her from the very start that he wasn't going to be hanging around and his conscience would be clear.

He'd approached all his relationships with the opposite sex like that. With honesty and no promises. If some of them had become distraught when he'd walked away because they'd been pointlessly looking for more than he had in him to give, then so be it. Not his fault. How could it have been when he'd done nothing but warned them off going down that road?

But the situation with Rose was different and that was something he had failed to factor in.

He'd conveniently whitewashed the whole business of *why* he had turned up, unannounced, on her doorstep into something that wasn't really relevant—he wasn't going to be sticking around so she would never actually discover his true identity. Therefore, why did it matter *who* he was?

Except it did.

And now he would have to pay the price for his not-so-innocent deception.

It was not quite six in the evening. He had spent the day partly in the library, where he had worked in pleasurable peace, and partly in a five-star hotel near Oxford, where a high-level meeting had been arranged with the CEO of a company he intended to buy.

He wondered whether his attack of conscience had been kick-started by that return to the reality of his high-powered city life. Sitting at that table, back in his comfort zone of work, business and making money... had it brought him back down to earth with a bump? Reminded him of the single tenet he had always lived by—work was the only thing upon which a person could rely?

Art didn't know. He just knew that he owed Rose more than a disappearing act.

He made it back to her house within fifteen minutes, to find her still in her office alone, Phil having gone for the day.

Rose looked up and smiled.

He'd told her that he didn't do commitment and he didn't do domesticity and yet they'd cooked together and discussed everything under the sun from world politics to village gossip.

'You're just in time,' she said, standing up and stretching. 'If I read any more of this file I'm going to end up banging my head on the desk in frustration. You wouldn't believe the spurious arguments this company is using to get rid of one of their longest-serving employees just because it would be cheaper for them to get a young person on board.'

'The world of the underdog would be nothing without you...' Art framed that light-hearted rejoinder in a voice that lacked his customary self-assurance.

He clenched his fists, walked towards the double-fronted bay window, sat down on the ledge and stared out for a few silent seconds.

'Are you disappointed in the outcome of the protest?' he asked abruptly, swinging around to look at her but remaining where he was by the window, perched on the broad ledge, his legs loosely crossed.

He had no idea how to begin this conversation and even less idea as to where it was going to end. For once in his life he was freefalling without a safety net and he loathed the sensation.

For a man to whom control was vitally important, this lack of control was his worst nightmare.

Rose tilted her head to one side. The smile with which she had greeted him had faded because she was sensing that something was out of kilter, although she wasn't sure what.

'Not disappointed, no...' She gave his question consideration. 'I always knew it was going to be a token protest because the land had been bought and all the channels had been navigated with planning permission, but I do think it's a result if the developers consent to all the things they've made noises about.'

'They will.'

'You seem very sure about that.' Rose laughed because this sort of assertiveness was just typical of him and it was something she really...

For a few seconds her heart stopped beating and she could feel the prickle of perspiration break out over her body. Something she *really found amusing.* Not something she *loved*, but something she found *amusing.*

'I am.'

'Well, I must say, it would be fantastic for the community as a whole. Naturally, I still stand by my guns when I say that I hate big developers who think they can descend and gobble up whatever slice of land they want, but it's fair to say that not many would go the extra mile to appease disgruntled locals.'

Art didn't say anything. He'd slept with her and done a hundred small things with her that he'd never done with anyone else. That, in itself, was unsettling and he latched onto that sentiment with some relief because it made him realise that he was clearing off in the nick of time. Sharing cosy suppers and painting bedrooms wasn't in his genetic make-up and never would be! He wasn't cut out for anything like that and had he stayed on he knew that the inevitable boredom with her would have set in.

She invigorated him *at this moment in time*, but it wouldn't have lasted.

He would have become restless, got itchy feet. It never failed to happen.

Which was *why*, he thought with conviction, it was imperative he left. Rose, underneath the tough veneer, had risen above the odds dealt to her in her background and turned out to be endearingly romantic. Were he to stay on, there was a chance that she would have fallen for him.

And then what? A broken heart when he vanished? A life in need of being rebuilt? Looking at the bigger picture, he was doing her a favour.

'That's because,' Art told her patiently, 'there's always more to people than meets the eye, and that includes billionaire developers.'

'Really? I hadn't noticed. Do you want to tell me what's going on here, Art, or shall I make it easier for you by bringing it out into the open myself?'

'What do you mean?' He frowned.

'I mean you...*this atmosphere*...' She breathed in deeply and exhaled slowly. 'Something's off and I'll spare you the discomfort of spelling it out in words of one syllable, shall I? You're leaving. Your time here is up. You came for a protest that ended up a damp squib. Perhaps you were hoping for more fireworks.'

'The opposite,' Art told her quietly.

'You're...not off?'

'No, that bit you got right. I... It's time for me to pack my bags and leave.'

Rose stared at him, horrified at how painful it was to hear those words. Everywhere hurt. He was going. She'd known he'd be off but, now that he'd confirmed it, it felt as though she'd been hit head-on by a train. Her legs had turned to jelly but she kept standing, holding her ground and hoping with everything inside her that the pain tearing her apart wasn't reflected in her face.

'Of course,' she said politely.

'You always knew I'd be leaving.'

'Because you're a wanderer in search of a cause.'

'Not entirely.'

'What do you mean? What are you talking about?'

'I think this is a conversation better conducted with you sitting down.'

'Why?' Rose wondered whether she would be able to move at all without falling to the ground in an undignified heap. That was what jelly legs did to a person.

'Because...you might find what I'm about to say somewhat surprising.'

Rose looked at him uncertainly, then galvanised her body into action. She wasn't going to sit at her desk. She wasn't conducting an interview! Although the atmosphere felt hardly less formal.

She walked towards the sitting room, which was the only room downstairs, aside from the large cloakroom, that hadn't been converted into something useful that could be modified and used as a source of income.

Like all the other rooms in the house, it was high-ceilinged and gracious in proportions. It was painted in soothing shades of grey and cream and lavender and the furniture was well-made and tasteful.

Rose flopped down onto the sofa and then watched in tense silence as he prowled the room, his beautiful lean body jerky as he darted thoughtful glances in her direction.

'Are you going to spare us both the drama and just say what you have to say? It's not as though you haven't warned me in advance and you needn't worry that I'm going to do anything silly like break down and cry.'

'It might be better if I show you,' Art said slowly. He pulled out his phone, found what he was looking for on the screen and handed it to her. And waited, eyes glued to her expressive face. Every nerve in his body twanged with the sort of tension he had seldom experienced in his life before.

He watched as bewilderment turned to confusion, as confusion turned to disbelief and then, finally, as disbelief morphed into appalled horror.

Long after she should have finished reading the article about him, just one of many to be found online, she kept staring at the phone as though hopeful that it might deliver something that would make sense of what he'd shown her.

His biography. Succinct. Replete with his success stories. Sycophantic in its adoration of the man who had made his first billion before the ripe old age of thirty-five.

She finally looked up with a dazed expression.

'*You're* DC Logistics…?'

Art flushed darkly but he wasn't going to start justifying himself.

'Yes,' he said flatly.

'*You're* the guy we've been fighting…'

'Yes.'

'You came here… You pretended to be… *Why*?' She shot up, trembling, as thousands of implications clearly began sinking in. 'You *bastard*.' She edged away from him, recoiling as though he was contagious, and took up position by the large Victorian fireplace, leaning against it and staring at him with huge round eyes.

'You came here with a plan, didn't you? You came here so that you could infiltrate and get us onside. You didn't like the fact that we were protesting about you putting up a bunch of houses that no one wants!'

Art's jaw hardened but there was nothing he could say to refute her accusations since they were all spot on. 'I owned the land. I was going to build, whether you stood in the way or not. I thought it diplomatic to try to persuade you to see sense before the bulldozers moved in and trying to persuade you within the walls of my London offices wasn't going to work.'

'You *used* me.'

'I…' Art raked his fingers through his hair. 'There was no need for me to come clean. And I did not *use* you. We both enjoyed what happened between us. I could have walked away without saying anything.'

'Are you asking for a medal because you finally decided to tell the truth?'

'There was also no need for me to grant the concessions that I have.'

'No wonder you were so confident that the big, bad developers were going to accept our terms and conditions. Because *you* were the big, bad developer.'

'I played fair.'

'You lied!'

'A small amount of subterfuge.'

'You came here…you…' She turned away because she needed to gather herself. Everything was rushing in on her and she was beginning to feel giddy. She took a few deep breaths and forced herself to look at him. To her fury, he met her gaze squarely, as if he was as pure as the driven snow!

'I let you stay in my house.' Rose laughed bitterly. 'No wonder you insisted on paying rent! You're worth a small fortune. It must have troubled your conscience that you were sponging off someone who couldn't hope to come close to matching you in the financial stakes. Someone with rooms in need of decorating and plumbing on the verge of waving a white flag and giving up! I bet you've never painted anything in your life before or done anything manual *at all*!'

'Going through each and every detail of the ways you feel deceived isn't going to progress this.'

'I slept with you.'

Those four words, delivered without any expression

whatsoever, dropped like stones into a quiet pond and silence settled between them, thick and uncomfortable.

'I'm guessing...' Rose kept her voice level but the blood was rushing through her veins like lava '...that that was all part of the game plan? To get me onside?'

'That's outrageous!'

'Really? Is it? Why? You conned your way into my home!'

'I was more than happy to go stay in a hotel.'

'You accepted my hospitality and you *used it* to get what you wanted out of me! I can't believe I was stupid enough to actually think that you were a man of integrity.'

'Sleeping with you was never part of any plan.' Art shook his head and dropped down on the sofa, legs apart. She walked towards him and stood in front of him with her arms folded. 'You doubt me?' he growled, staring at her, and even in the height of this scorching argument, when she was burning with rage, those fabulous dark eyes still had the power to do things to her body. Rose's lips thinned.

'Do you honestly believe that I could make love with you the way I have if I wasn't seriously attracted to you?'

Hot colour flooded her cheeks. Rose remembered the intensity of their lovemaking, the flaring passion in his eyes. She remembered the way he had touched her, his fingers as they'd explored her body and the urgency of those times when he just couldn't wait to have her.

No, he hadn't been faking *that*. Somehow that was

something she just knew. He'd come here on a mission but going to bed with her had never been part of the plan. Should she feel better for that? Maybe, but then, with a bitter twist, she also remembered the way *she* had felt about *him* and her stupidity in actually thinking that there might have been more to what they had than just a romp in the sack.

It was *always* going to be just a romp in the sack, had she but known, because she had *always* just been an enjoyable add-on to the main reason he was there, a pleasant side dish but never the main meal.

Humiliation roared through her, stiffening her backbone and settling like venom in her veins.

How on earth could she have been so stupid? She, of all people! Always cautious, always watchful…how could she have thrown herself in the path of a speeding train and actually thought that it would be okay?

'You need to leave,' she said coldly.

'I was honest with you.' Art rose to his feet, a towering, dominant presence that made her step back in alarm.

He sucked the oxygen out of the room, left her feeling as though she needed to gasp for air, and the strength of her reaction terrified her because she knew that, mixed in with the rage, the hatred and the bitter disillusionment, was something else…something she didn't want to put her finger on.

'And now that I'm weeping with gratitude at your terrific display of honesty, are you going to renege on all the things you said you'd do for the village?'

'Dammit, Rose!' Art roared. 'I could have just disappeared. Instead, I came clean. Why can't you cut me some slack?' He stepped towards her, ignoring her crab-like shuffle away from him, until he had cornered her without her even realising it was happening.

She collided with the wall and he placed both hands squarely on either side of her so that she had nowhere to run.

'I didn't come here to—' he looked away and clenched his jaw in frustration '—mess you or anyone else around.'

'You came here to get on our good side so that we would get off your case and make things easier for you!'

'Where's the crime in that? I purchased the land going through all the proper channels. Okay, yes, I admit I figured that life would be a lot smoother if I didn't have to steamroller my way through protesters waving placards, but I can't think of many *big, bad wolves* who would have given a damn about the pro-testers *or* their placards.'

'You could have done the decent thing and been hon-est from the start!'

'You would have had the sheriff run me out of town before I got the first sentence out.'

'That's not true.'

'Isn't it?'

Rose flushed. She could breathe him in and it was doing all sorts of crazy and unacceptable things to her nervous system.

'I thought,' Art said heavily, 'that this would be fairly straightforward. How hard could it be to talk sense into a group of people who were never going to win the war?

I never banked on really engaging with anyone here and I certainly never entertained the idea that...'

Rose tilted her chin and stared at him in hostile defiance. 'That what? That you'd break that code of yours and start sharing space in a kitchen with a woman?'

To think that she had actually entertained the idea that having him do all that domesticated stuff might be an indication of feelings that ran deeper and truer than they had both originally predicted.

'Something like that,' Art muttered, glancing away for a few taut seconds before returning his dark gaze to her face. 'You're hurt and I get that,' he continued in a low, driven voice.

Rose raised her eyebrows. She was keeping it together by a thread, determined not to let him see just how devastated she was, but it was so, so very hard, especially when he was standing so, so very close to her, when, with barely any effort, she could just reach out and touch that body she had come to feel so much for. Too much.

'Thanks. I feel so much better for that,' she said with thick sarcasm.

'I'm no good for you.' He gave her a crooked smile and pushed himself away, although he remained standing in front of her.

'No, you're not,' Rose said shortly.

'You deserve a far better man.'

'I do.' She tossed her hair and for a few seconds her expression changed from anger to on-the-edge-of-tears disappointment. 'I always knew that guys with money were unscrupulous and I proved myself right.'

'I refuse to get into a debate about this. I don't think

your fellow locals will agree when they find themselves the recipients of some spanking-new additions to the village. I don't think they'll be gnashing their teeth and shaking their fists and cursing my generosity.'

'You can wave money around but that doesn't make you an honourable man. It doesn't mean that you've got any sense of...of *spirituality.*'

'I didn't think you were paying too much attention to my fascinating lack of a spiritual side when we were in bed together.'

'How dare you bring that up?' The silence that greeted this was electric. Her nostrils flared and her pupils dilated and every pore in her body burned with humiliation because the warmth between her legs wouldn't let her forget the shameful truth that she still found him unbearably sexy even though she absolutely loathed him for how he had played her.

She breathed deep and closed her eyes and wasn't aware that he was reaching out until he was. Reaching out to lightly stroke the side of her face.

'You still want me,' he murmured and Rose glared at him furiously. 'You still want me and you can't deny it.'

Rose opened her mouth to utter an instant denial of any such thing. How dared he? Her skin burnt from where he had touched her. *How dared he?*

'Are you going to lie?' Art asked in a low, sexy undertone. 'You can't possibly stand there and accuse me of being a monster of deceit only to lie about something that's so obvious.'

'Well, it doesn't matter,' she said on a sharply indrawn breath. 'So what if I'm attracted to you? You're an attractive man. But I will never be tempted to act on that attraction again, not that the situation is ever likely to arise.' She took a deep breath. 'I can't fault you for being honest and telling me from the start that you weren't going to be sticking around. Fair enough. But you hurt me with your deceit, whether that deceit was intended or not. I'll never, ever forgive you for that.'

Art's lips thinned.

'Forgiveness has never been high on the list I've striven for.'

'Can I ask you something before you disappear back to that jet-set life of yours?' Rose folded her arms, proud of the fact that her voice continued to betray nothing of what was going on inside her, the roil of tumultuous emotions tearing her up.

'I'm guessing that's a question you will ask whatever my response.'

'If we'd stood firm, would you have steamrolled us all away? So that you could have your acres and acres of land for the sake of a handful of flash houses?'

'Yes.'

Rose frowned because she had sensed something behind that flat monosyllabic reply. A curious shadow had crossed his face but then she wondered whether she'd imagined it because when he fixed his deep, dark eyes on her they were as remote as hers were. Two people who had shared intimacies she had never dreamed of and now here they were, standing opposite one another with a huge unsurmountable wall between them.

Rose looked away quickly because she could feel the treacherous onset of tears.

She put distance between them and gathered herself.

'I'll get my things,' Art said abruptly. 'I'll be fifteen minutes, tops.'

'I expect you won't need to borrow my battered car to get you to the station? Maybe you could call your personal chauffeur to swing by for you. Or, if that's not efficient enough, I'm sure you could find a corner of your field to land a private jet.'

'My driver is on his way.'

'Of course he is,' Rose said acidly. 'I'll leave you to get on with your packing. You know where the front door is.'

She didn't look back. She headed straight to her office and she made sure to close and lock the door behind her. But she didn't cry. She knew how to contain the tears. She'd learned that trick at a very young age.

CHAPTER SEVEN

SITTING AT THE head of the conference table, around which twenty people were all looking to him, Art could feel nothing but a certain amount of apathy even though a deal that would harvest several million was on the verge of completion.

With some surprise, he realised that he had doodled Rose's company logo onto his legal pad, a detail he wasn't even aware he had stored in his memory bank.

He'd last seen her three weeks ago and the memory of that final encounter was one that he rehashed on a daily basis.

It was getting on his nerves.

His concentration levels were down. His focus was erratic. He'd made two dates with women. The first he'd managed to stick out for an hour or so before admitting defeat and making up an excuse to leave early. The second he'd simply bailed on before subjecting himself to the possibility of another evening of torturous banalities.

He dreamed of Rose.

Not only did the memory of her haunt his waking

hours, but it didn't have the decency to allow him to get a good night's sleep when he fell into bed in the early hours of the morning.

Art had come around to thinking that she had taken up residence in his head because things had not ended *properly* between them.

He'd left still wanting her and, like an itch that needed to be scratched, that *want* kept clamouring for satisfaction.

It didn't help that he'd also left knowing that *she* still wanted *him.*

It was frustrating because he had never had any area of his life over which he was unable to exercise complete control. In this instance it had gradually dawned on him that he would never get her out of his system unless he took her to bed once again.

Pride dictated that he drop all seditious thoughts along those lines. Common sense warned him away. The litany of complications if they ended up in bed again was too long to catalogue and it beggared belief that she would actually *want* to sleep with him anyway. Yes, she fancied him. She'd admitted that much. But her amazing eyes had been full of scorn even as the admission had been leaving her lips.

When Art thought about that, he felt a spurt of raw frustration that left him confused and at odds with himself. He wondered whether this was what it felt like to be dumped, a situation he had never personally had to endure.

He went through the motions for the remainder of the

morning. The deal was signed. His company's bank account was inflated to even more impossible proportions.

None of that touched him. What *did* affect him was when, two and a half hours later, he dialled Rose's number and sat back in his office chair, waiting to see whether she would ignore his call or pick up. His name would flash on her screen, warning her of his identity. Whatever she did now would dictate the way he responded. He would leave it to fate.

For the first time in weeks, Art felt comfortable. He was doing *something*. Circumstances hadn't simply conspired to yank the rug from under his feet and leave him feeling at odds with himself, restless and unable to concentrate.

The slate had been wiped clean. There were no more half-truths between them. He would see her. He would feel out the situation and then, who knew...?

Life was an unfolding mystery.

He heard her voice and automatically straightened, all senses on full alert, every primitive instinct honing in to what he wanted to do, where he wanted to go with this...

'Been a while,' he drawled, relaxing back in his chair and swivelling it so that he could stretch his legs out.

Rose had debated whether or not to take the call. His name had flashed up on the screen and her insides had immediately turned to mush even though, over the past long three weeks, she had played and replayed in her mind how she would react if he got in touch.

'What can I do for you?' she asked coolly.

'Surprised to hear from me?'

'Are you phoning about anything in particular, Art? Because I'm quite busy at the moment.'

'I'm almost there, finalising the details of my investment in your community.'

'I wouldn't know. I've handed that over to a property lawyer in Oxford, who is a close friend of mine. I'm sure he would be happy to supply details of the ongoing process but I've told him that there's no need to fill me in until everything's sorted.' Images of Art jumped into her head, sickly reminding her of the powerful and dramatic effect he had on her body. Even the sound of his voice was enough to make her breasts tingle and her breath shorten.

'I rather think,' Art drawled, 'that I would like *you* to be personally involved in the closure of all of this.'

'Me? What? *Why?*'

'You started it, in a manner of speaking. It's only fair that you should finish it. Aside from which, if I'm to sink a vast sum of money into the community, it would benefit from someone knowing the place first-hand, knowing where best to divide the cash and how to put it to the best possible use. I may be generous, but I'm not a pushover. I have no intention of seeing my money ineptly spent on whatever takes some councillor's fancy. So handing over the file to someone else to tie up all the loose ends isn't doing it for me.'

'I haven't got time.'

What would it involve? She surely wouldn't have to meet him again! She couldn't face it. It was bad enough hearing the deep, dark, sexy timbre of his voice down the end of a phone line. She couldn't get her head around the possibility of actually ever seeing him in the flesh. He'd deceived her and he'd slept with her, knowing all the time that whilst she had been opening up to him, which was a big deal for her, she'd been opening up to a stranger.

'Well, then, you'll have to make time.' Art sliced through that objection swiftly and conclusively. 'You've turned caring for the community into an art form, Rose. It's not asking too much for you to step up to the plate and finish the job. When can you get to London so that we can discuss this?'

'*We?*' Rose queried faintly, as her stomach fell away and her mouth dried.

'Why, me and you, of course,' Art said in a tone of incredulity that she should even have thought to ask such an obvious question. 'I can't very well ask you to finish the job when I don't do likewise, can I? My people have handled all the formalities. We can agree the sign-off. And I think it would be beneficial for you to have a look at the details of the houses I intend to build on the land.'

'But I don't see why.' Rose cleared her throat, anxiously wondering what would happen if she flat-out refused. Would he renege on the deal? No! She knew he wasn't that sort but the possibility still niggled. It would be a disaster because he now had the complete, enthusiastic backing of everyone in the community and if it all collapsed because of her then she would be mortified.

'I don't see the point of another lengthy explanation. Now, when can you get down here? I wouldn't suggest commuting—I think you should plan on having a couple of days in London. There are legalities we can iron out between us and I will need to see some plans for the distribution of my money. In fact, it wouldn't be remiss of me to suggest a week. I can arrange for a makeshift office to be set up at my headquarters in the city if you need to spend some time communicating with clients. Or you could always take a bit of holiday. Enjoy the sights. It's quite different to the countryside.'

'Get down there? London? And yes, Art, I *do* realise that the big city is a little different to a field of cows and a village with a post office, a corner shop and a pub in case anyone wants a nightlife.'

'Not my thoughts and certainly not my words. I have my diary to hand. I could block out some time from the day after tomorrow. It won't be easy but the sooner this business is wrapped up the better, and construction can start on the land. And I won't remind you that any delay to the work beginning is a mere formality and a courtesy to you.'

Rose detected the crispness in his voice and pictured him glancing at his watch, raring to get on with more important business. He was doing what he felt was the right thing, involving her in the final process, and what he said made sense. She had supported the protesters and it was only fair to them and to the community that she take an active part in deciding how the money should be distributed to best benefit everyone.

She was overreacting because of the tumult of emotions that still coursed through her at the thought of him.

It wasn't like that for Art. He had taken a bit of time out with her but he was back where he belonged and she would be no more than a fast-fading memory for him. If she did what she wanted to do, namely launch into a thousand reasons why she had no intention of having anything further to do with a man who had deceived her, he wouldn't understand. He had given her his reasons for having done what he had, he had come clean and frankly, as far as he was concerned, had elevated himself to the position of self-proclaimed saint because he could have just walked away, leaving her none the wiser. What was the big deal now? All water under the bridge.

Playing it as cool as he was, she thought, was the only way to deal with the situation and maybe, just maybe, seeing him again and in a different environment would kill off the effect he continued to have on her, against all reason.

He would be in his natural habitat. He would be surrounded by all those trappings of wealth that she had never had time for in the past. Plus, speed would be of the essence for him. He wanted the whole business sorted fast. A couple of days in his company might be just the thing for clearing her head because ever since he'd disappeared she'd done nothing but think of him and the longing, the anger, the disenchantment and the regret were wreaking havoc with her sleep and distracting her from her work.

Bucked up by this process of reasoning, Rose felt a little calmer when she answered.

'If you hold for a minute, I'll check my schedule…'

* * *

Art held. For a minute, two minutes...when he looked at his watch with some impatience it was to find that she had kept him hanging on for five minutes. Inconceivable. He gritted his teeth and wondered what he would do if she turned him down flat, as she had every right to do. He could waffle on about the importance of both of them jointly putting the finishing touches to the deal that had been brokered to ease acceptance of the construction of his development, but any close inspection would reveal more holes in that argument than a colander.

'Well?' he pressed.

'Okay.'

'Okay?' Art straightened, a slashing smile of intense satisfaction softening his lean face. 'Good. Tell me when, exactly, you will be arriving and I will make sure that suitable accommodation is sorted for you.'

'I can sort my own accommodation,' Rose asserted hurriedly.

'You're not paying for a hotel.'

'No way am I...'

'I believe this is a favour it is within my remit to return,' Art said flatly, cutting her off in mid-protest, 'and, just in case you're thinking of a speech about accepting favours from me, let me assure you that no money will leave my hands.'

'What do you mean?'

'I own the hotel.'

'Of course you do,' Rose snapped. 'I wonder why I'm not surprised at that. I did look you up online but the list of things you owned was so long that I fell asleep before I could get to the end. I didn't get to the hotel.'

'Chain.'

'I beg your pardon?'

'Hotel *chain*. A little sideline I invested in some years ago that has ended up exceeding all expectations.'

'Good for you. I shudder to think what must have gone through your head when you were confronted with a paintbrush, a can of paint and four walls with peeling plaster.'

Art burst out laughing. 'It was an unforeseen challenge. Now, back to business. Do you require somewhere to work? And, before you say no, I'll tell you again that it would be no trouble for me to have someone arrange an office for you.'

'It would be helpful,' Rose said through her no doubt gritted teeth. 'With a bit of juggling, I shall try to arrange a couple of client visits while I'm in London. It would work if I could have somewhere to go with them. And, of course, at some point I'll have to see Anton.'

'Anton?' Art's ears pricked up and he frowned.

'Anton Davies. He's the lawyer who has been handling the formalities in Oxford. If there's going to be a transition of duties then we'll have to get together to discuss that and to work out his fee accordingly. Although…he's not the sort to quibble.'

Art heard the smile in her voice, the softening of her tone, and his hackles rose accordingly.

But, he thought, if she was working under his roof, so to speak, then he could easily find his way to whatever space had been allocated to her and meet the guy.

It was a taste of jealousy rarely experienced and he moved on from that to conclude the conversation.

Less than five minutes later, everything had been sorted. It took one phone call to his PA for the hotel room to be arranged and a work space sorted.

She was going to experience the joy of five-star luxury and the seclusion of an office in one of the most prestigious buildings in the city.

He sat back and luxuriated in a feeling of pure satisfaction that was very far from the cool, forbidding and controlled exterior he showed the world.

Rose had no idea really what to expect of her time in London. She had been all cool logic and common sense ever since she had agreed to Art's proposal but now, standing in front of the daunting glass tower where his headquarters was housed, her heart plummeted faster than a boulder dropped from a great height.

At her side was her pull-along case, neatly packed with essentials. Work clothes. Prim, proper work clothes which were nothing like the relaxed, informal stuff she was accustomed to wearing in her own house. The image she wanted to project was one of inaccessible businesslike efficiency. There was no way she wanted him to think for a passing minute that she was the same woman who had hopped into bed with him, breathless and girly and excited.

To that end, she had actually bought two reasonably priced grey skirts and a jacket, two white blouses and a pair of black pumps. The perfect wardrobe for a woman who was in London for business.

She was wearing a sensible white bra which matched her sensible white knickers and bolstered her self-confidence as she continued to gaze at the aggressively thrusting glass facade with a racing heart.

She had asked for a schedule and a schedule she had duly received. Arrival at ten. She would then be shown to her temporary working quarters and then taken to the hotel, where she would deposit her belongings. At that point she could choose to return to the office to work if she liked. In all events, she wouldn't be seeing Art until early evening in his office, where they would briefly discuss some of the details of the projects that lay ahead for the village.

She had liaised with his personal assistant by email for all of this and, reading between the lines, she had got the message that Arturo da Costa, billionaire and legend in the world of business and finance, was a man who had precious little time to spare so what she was getting would be his leftover free time, a few snatched moments here and there when he happened not to be closing an important deal or entertaining important big shots.

Rose had held her tongue and refrained from pointing out the obvious. Why on earth was he bothering to see her at all if he was *that* busy? But then she remembered that he was the guy who had gone the extra mile to appease the natives and this was just a duty-bound finishing touch to his benevolence.

Anyway, she thought now, taking a deep breath and propelling herself into the glass tower, it was great that he was only going to be around now and again.

That way, she would see enough of him to kill all the foolish, nostalgic, whimsical memories that seemed to have dogged her, against all her better judgement. She would have a world class view of the real man and he wasn't going to be the easy-going, sexy, laid-back guy who had painted a room in her house and stood by her side in the kitchen pretending that he knew what to do when it came to food preparation, joking and teasing and turning her on just by being *him*.

A little disorientated, she found herself in a vast marble-floored foyer, manned by an army of receptionists who would not have looked out of place in *Vogue* magazine and, just in case anyone might think that there was an unfair proportion of female models in front of those silver terminals and where the heck was feminism when you wanted it, then they'd have to think again because there was a fair sprinkling of men alongside them who also looked as though they'd have been quite at home on a catwalk. People were coming and going. There was an air of purpose about the place. This was what the business of vast money-making looked like. It was as far removed from her own workplace as an igloo was from a hut on a tropical beach.

She had no idea who would be meeting her but she was expecting the helpful PA.

She was certainly not expecting Art and, indeed, was unaware of him until she heard his voice behind her, deep and dark and sexy.

'You're here.'

Rose spun around. She'd gone from ice cold to

scorching hot in the space of two seconds. Dazed, she focused on him and the heat pouring through her body almost made her pass out.

'I wasn't sure whether you were going to come or not,' Art remarked, already turned on even though the deliberately uninspiring office outfit should have been enough to snuff out any stirrings of ardour.

It was her face. It had haunted him and one look at her revived every single image that had been floating around in his head and every single lustful thought that had accompanied those images.

He was pleased that he had been proactive. He could have sat around thinking of her. Sooner or later the memories would have vanished into the ether but he wasn't a man to rely on a *sooner or later* scenario.

The interruption to the smooth flow of his work life had been intolerable and the solution he had engineered had been worth the trouble.

Art hadn't known how he was going to play his cards when she arrived. He'd acted on impulse in engineering the situation in the first place, had ceded to the demands of his body.

Now, for the first time in his life, he was taking a chance and venturing into unknown territory. At an age when he should have been having fun, Art had had to grow up fast to deal with his father's unpredictable behaviour and the emotional and financial fallout each relationship had left in its wake. Before he had had a chance to plot his own life, he had already concluded that the only safe course was to hold tight to his emotions and to his money. Lose control and he could end up like his father. Adrift and ripped off.

This was the biggest chance he had ever taken. At least he wasn't going to be ripped off and she would be gone just as soon as he got this *thing* out of his system.

He still wanted her. He accepted that as his body surged into hot arousal. Didn't make sense but there you had it. What they had required a natural conclusion and looking at her now, seeing the way her cheeks reddened and noting the slight tremble in her hands, Art knew that she felt the same.

Even if she didn't know it. Yet.

He dealt her a slow smile of utter charm and Rose's mouth tightened.

'Well, here I am,' she replied neutrally. She wondered whether that remark of his had hinted at a suspicion that she might have tried to avoid meeting him because of the effect he still had on her. Had he thought that she had hesitated because she'd been scared of seeing him again? Or was that just being fanciful?

The way he was looking at her…

She dropped her eyes and resisted the temptation to fidget. 'I was under the impression that your secretary would be meeting me.'

'Change of plan.'

'Why?' She looked at him and it took a lot of willpower not to instantly look away because gazing into those fathomless dark eyes was the equivalent of having a shock delivered to her nervous system.

'Call it respect for the fact that what we had was bigger than the sum total of what I'm going to contribute to your community.'

Rose felt the sting of colour creep into her cheeks. She didn't want the past recalled. She wanted the brief time they'd shared neatly boxed up and shoved somewhere out of sight.

'There was no need,' she said tightly. 'I'm not here to have a stroll down memory lane, Art. It's not appropriate. I'm here to sort whatever details need sorting and then I'm heading back home. The quicker we can deal with what we need to decide the better.'

'In which case,' Art said briskly, 'let's start with your work space…'

It was the same size as the room which she shared with Phil and their assistant and all the various people who came and went at will. Compared with the clutter of the office in her house, the clean white modernist vision she had been allocated made her jaw drop.

She thought of the warm chaos of her own house and the familiar sounds of occupied rooms and felt a pang of longing so great that it took her breath away.

Life pre-Art had been simple. Making ends meet as she'd buried herself in her worthwhile causes had been a walk in the park because, when it came to stress, there was nothing more stressful than dealing with emotions. She had managed to avoid that for her entire life because no one had ever penetrated the protective wall she had built around herself.

'What is it?'

'Nothing,' Rose muttered, looking down at her feet.

'Don't you like the office space?'

He'd moved directly in front of her and Rose only managed to stand her ground through sheer willpower and a driving urge not to feel intimidated.

'It's very...nice.'

'Very *nice*?' Art looked away briefly, then returned his dark searching gaze to her face.

'It's not what I'm used to.' Rose cleared her throat and gathered herself. 'It really makes me see the gaping chasm between us.'

Art flushed darkly. 'We've been over this. Let me take you to the hotel. You can drop your bag and then we'll go for lunch.'

'Art, there's no need to put yourself out for me. I don't expect you to take me to lunch or anywhere else, for that matter. Your PA gave me the impression that I wouldn't actually be seeing a great deal of you.'

'Like I said, plans change. You'll be thrilled to hear that I've cleared my diary for you.'

Rose looked at him wryly, eyebrows raised. 'Do I look thrilled?'

'I've missed your sense of humour. Some men might be turned off because you're not simpering, but not me.' Art held her gaze and raked his fingers through his dark hair, his lean body taut and tense.

Rose stilled. Her whole body froze and for a few seconds she wondered whether she had heard correctly. His fabulous eyes were giving nothing away but there was something there that made her mouth go dry.

'You *missed* me?'

Her body came to life. Her nipples pinched and a

spreading dampness between her legs was a painful reminder of the dramatic effect he still had on her.

She'd hoped that seeing him in his gilded surroundings would kill off what remnants of idiotic sexual attraction lingered inside her, but looking at him now...

She was no expert but that suit looked handmade, to match the shoes which also looked handmade. His smooth, ridiculously sophisticated attire would probably have cost the equivalent of what most normal earthlings earned in a year. It should have got up her nose, been a massive turn-off, and yet she had a sudden urge to swoon.

'Well, I have not missed *you*,' she croaked and he looked at her steadily, eyes pinned to her flustered face. 'And I don't appreciate you...bringing this up. What happened between us...happened and I'm not here to rake up the past. As I've already told you.'

'I know. I'm crashing through all those barriers and voicing what you don't want to hear.'

'Shall I be honest with you?' He dropped the loaded question into the lengthening silence and waited.

'No,' she whispered.

'I still want you, Rose. Just standing here is doing all sorts of things to my body, turning it on in ways you couldn't begin to imagine. You're in my system and, I won't lie, you're screwing up my working life because I can't get you out of my head.'

'Art, don't...' Rose heard the weak tremble in her voice with horror. She glanced at him and her breath hitched in her throat.

'I still want you in my bed,' he continued roughly.

'It's the only way I can think of to get you out of my system. I won't lay a finger on you but…every time you look at me, you should know that I'm thinking about touching you.' He stared away.

'I should never have come here!'

'But you're here now. Do you want to leave?' His smouldering dark eyes fastened on her, pinning her to the spot.

Rose hesitated. As he said, she was here now and she would sort out all the fine detail he had summoned her to London to sort out. She had promised all those loyal protestors that she would return with plans in place for them to start thinking long-term about improvements to the community. She wasn't going to let them down.

'I'll do what I came here to do,' she replied, breathing in deep and not looking away. 'I told everyone I would have details for them to pick over and I have no intention of going back empty-handed. What you think when you look at me is your business.'

CHAPTER EIGHT

IF ART HAD planned on dropping a bomb in her life then he'd succeeded.

He still wanted her. He still wanted to take her to his bed. He still wanted to do all those things to her that she still wanted to do to him.

When Rose thought about that she felt giddy. She knew that, by being honest, he had deliberately dropped that bomb to wreak havoc with her peace of mind. Honest or selfish? Did he really care if he ended up getting what he wanted? He'd got her to London under false pretences and now he was playing a waiting game.

It had only been forty-eight hours but already her nerves were shredded. She felt like a minnow being slowly circled by a shark and, worse, the minnow was finding it hard to stop fantasising about its predator.

Now, he was taking her out to an elaborate dinner.

'Networking,' he had explained succinctly, having earlier dropped by her office, which had also turned into her sanctuary, where she could find a brief reprieve from his overwhelming personality.

She had looked up and given him a perplexed frown,

which had clearly done nothing to dampen his high spirits.

'I'm not here to network.'

'Granted, but this is a charity event hosted by some fairly prominent members of the international legal community. All those causes you take such an interest in? Well, they'll be represented across the board. Several people you'll have heard of will also be giving speeches and, for the intrepid, I gather there will be an opportunity to go abroad to places where civil liberties are at risk. You may not want to personally vanish to the opposite side of the globe on a crusade to eradicate injustice, but you might be interested in meeting fellow like-minded citizens who are.'

'A charity event?'

'Reasonably smart, I should point out, as these things invariably are. A few degrees off black tie.'

'I haven't brought any smart clothes with me, Art.'

'Nothing but the *hands-off* suits that could have been designed to deter roving eyes and repel curious hands,' he murmured, in his first departure from the perfectly well-behaved gentleman he had been since his warning of intent. 'Why don't you get yourself something? You can charge it to my company account. Elaine, my PA, will sort that out for you.'

'I couldn't...'

He'd shrugged but he'd dropped the bait and she'd taken it.

How could she not?

Rose immediately told herself that it didn't mean anything. She'd been presented with an opportunity to meet people she admired so why shouldn't she grab the chance just because Art had arranged it? She could pat herself on the back for not letting his suffocating presence plunge her into a state of permanent confusion. And since he seemed convinced that she wouldn't take him up on his offer to subsidise an evening dress for the event, then why shouldn't she prove him wrong and do what he least expected?

Rose wasn't stupid. She knew how to sift through the deceit and ferret out the truth. Art had descended on their village with one thing in mind and that had been to persuade her to stop the protests that were slowing up development of the land he'd bought. He could have run roughshod over all of them because he had the law on his side but he was clever enough to know that a diplomatic solution would have been preferable and so that was the road he had decided to go down.

He hadn't banked on her being a nuisance and getting in his way but he'd found her attractive and she knew why. It was because she represented everything he wasn't accustomed to. From the way she dressed to the person that she was, she was a woman far removed from the stereotypes he was used to dating and he had found that appealing.

He went out with catwalk models. Nothing could have been further than a pro bono lawyer whose wardrobe consisted of flowing skirts, baggy tops, faded jeans and waterproof anoraks.

She'd been a trip down novelty lane and that hurt.

When Rose tried to equate that to her own feelings

towards him she drew a blank because she had been
drawn to him against all good reason.

It didn't make sense but everything about his personality had appealed to her. She'd been cautious but
in the end she hadn't been able to resist the pull of his
intelligence, his easy wit, his charm. Was she more like
her mother than she realised? It didn't matter whether
her mother had been a loyal wife. When her husband
had died she had behaved in a way that had had last-
ing consequences for her daughter. She had been pro-
miscuous and eventually she had ended up with a guy
who had been so out of her league that it was a mystery
that they had lasted as long as they had. Rose had been
careful all her life not to repeat any of the mistakes her
mother had made and it frightened her when she thought
of where she was now.

She had opened up to Art. Even before he had shown
his true colours, she had *known* that he wasn't the kind
of man who should have registered on her radar, but
she had *still* fallen for him and she had actually fooled
herself into thinking that *he* might have had similar
feelings for her.

Not so.

For Art, it was all about the sex, hence his openness
in telling her straight off the bat that he still wanted
her. Had she given off some kind of pheromone that
had alerted him to the fact that she still fancied him?

That horrified her but she was honest enough to realise that it had probably been the case because, the
second she was in his presence, her head and her body

took off in two different directions and she was left rudderless and floundering and he was a guy who could pick up on things like that in a heartbeat.

With her thoughts all over the place and her body threatening to go its own way and let the side down, Rose had gone to town shopping for something to wear to the charity event.

Part of her was determined to show him that she was more than just a country bumpkin lawyer with no dress sense.

Another part was curious to see whether, exposed to the sort of gathering that didn't frequently occur in her life out in the sticks, she would find that there were other interesting men out there. That Art hadn't netted all her attention to the exclusion of everyone else. Had he been as much of a novelty for her as she had been for him? Was she giving him too much credit for having burrowed into the heart of her when, in fact, she had just been vulnerable to a charming man because she'd been out of the dating scene for too long?

To this end, she had gone all out and now, with a mere forty minutes to go before Art's driver called for her, Rose contemplated her reflection in the floor-to-ceiling mirror with satisfaction.

In the background, she absently took in the sumptuous surroundings that had made her gasp the first time she had entered the hotel room. The lush curtains, the blonde wood, the pale marbled bathroom...the decadent chandelier that should have been over the top but wasn't...the handmade desk on which was stacked fine quality personalised stationery and a comprehensive collection of London guidebooks which she had had precious little time to peruse.

She refocused on her reflection.

She had gone for drama and chosen a figure-hugging dress in a striking shade of raspberry. The narrowness of her waist was emphasised by a silver corded belt that lent the outfit a Roman appeal and the dress fell elegantly to mid-calf. In nude heels, her legs looked longer and her body more willowy than she had ever noticed before.

And her hair. It fell in tousled waves along her shoulders and down her back and was as soft as silk because she had managed to squeeze in an appointment with a hairdresser, who had done some wonderful things with highlights and blow-dried it in a way she couldn't possibly have done herself.

She'd also bought a shawl in the same nude shade as the heels and she slung that over her shoulders and smiled, excited.

She felt like an exotic bird of paradise.

For the first time in her life, Rose wasn't being cautious. No, she amended, gathering all her stuff as her cell phone buzzed, alerting her to the arrival of the driver...

She'd already thrown caution to the winds when she'd jumped into bed with Art. She was just carrying on in a similar vein and enjoying herself in the process.

It was sufficient to bring a guilty tinge to her cheeks but she was composed as she slid into the back of the glossy Mercedes and she maintained that composure all the way to the venue and right up to the moment she spied Art, who was waiting for her, as arranged, in the lobby of the hotel.

Stepping out of the car, with the door held open by one of the parking attendants who had sprung into action the second the car had pulled up, made her feel like a movie star.

This was more than just *fancy*. There were journalists snapping pictures of the arriving guests. In a daze, she realised that she recognised faces from the world of movies and television and one or two prominent politicians and their other halves.

But all those faces faded into a blur alongside Art, who had begun moving towards her and, in the process, created a bubble of excitement around him.

He looked magnificent. The whiteness of his dress shirt emphasised his bronzed complexion. The black bow tie looked ridiculously sexy instead of stuffy, as did the very proper black suit.

Rose was barely aware of him moving to politely usher her inside.

'You look,' he breathed without looking at her and only inclining slightly so that he couldn't be overheard, 'sensational. Was that the intention?'

'Thank you. That's very kind.' But her pulse raced and she shivered with wild pleasure at his husky undertone.

Art laughed as they strolled away from the lobby and into the impressive ballroom, which was buzzing with the great and the good. 'Not a description that's been used much about me but I'll take it.'

'I mean it. Look at the women here.' She was holding onto him for dear life, very much aware that they were being stared at. 'I recognise some of them from fashion magazines.'

'And I thought that you never read anything as frivolous as a fashion magazine.'

'But thank you for pretending that I look okay,' Rose said distractedly.

'Where's this sudden attack of modesty sprung from?' They'd left the paparazzi outside; there was still a sea of people but without the gawping of the public and the reporters. Art drew her to the side and looked down at her. 'You're the most self-confident woman I've ever met.'

'When it comes to work…'

'You knock spots off every woman in this place.'

Rose burst out laughing. If he wanted to put her at ease, then he was doing a good job of it. 'I don't. But thanks.'

'You're fishing.'

'Of course I'm not!'

'You know how I feel about you. The only thing I want to do right now is get you out of here and into a bed so that I can make love to you until we're both too exhausted to carry on. I want to peel that dress off your luscious body and touch you in all the places I know you like being touched. So when I tell you that you put every other woman in the shade here, then trust me. I'm not kidding.'

'Stop!' Her blood was boiling and she was so very aware of him that she could barely think. 'You know I don't want you saying things like that…to me.'

'Say that like you mean it.'

'I *do* mean it. I'm just a little...nervous.'

'No need. Look around you. If you were hoping to attract some glances, then you've succeeded.' Art heard the edge in his voice and knew that it was a few degrees off the light, amused tone he had intended. *She* might not have noticed, but *he* had seen the way men had turned to have a second look. Most women were dressed to kill in black. Rose was a splash of exotic colour, a bird of paradise with her long wild hair and her strong intelligent face. She announced to the world that she was *different* and that was a very sexy trait. And not just to him.

Halfway through the evening, he realised that she had disappeared into the crowd. The man who was accustomed to a high level of irritation with women clinging like limpets to him at functions like this found that his irritation level was skyrocketing now and for a different reason.

Where the hell was she *now*? And why was he having to hunt for her?

It got on his nerves. She was a flash of red but, before he could pin her down, she was gone. Nursing a whisky while a blonde tried to get his attention, Art decided that, for Rose's own good, he would take her back to the hotel.

'Got to go.' He interrupted the blonde abruptly. Pushing himself away from the wall, against which he had been leaning, he ignored a couple of MPs who had been trying to gain his attention.

Rose was laughing at something some guy was telling her. Art wasn't born yesterday. He could recognise a man on the make a mile away.

He came to an abrupt towering halt in front of them and Rose blinked and frowned at him.

'Mind if I interrupt?' Art interrupted anyway. 'I've barely seen you all evening...'

'That's because I've been chatting to all the interesting people here,' Rose returned gaily, swiping a glass of wine from a passing waitress. 'For instance, this is Steve and he does some amazing work for the UN.'

Steve reddened and straightened and stuck out his hand, clearly awed by Art, who felt ancient and cynical beyond his years in comparison. He politely asked a couple of interested questions but his attention was focused on Rose and his body language dismissed the young fair-haired man, who duly evaporated into the crowd after boldly exchanging phone numbers with Rose.

Which made Art's teeth snap together with annoyance.

'I think it's time to go,' he said without preamble.

'But I'm not ready to leave yet.'

'Tough. It's been over four hours, which is two hours longer than I usually stay at these things.'

'I'm having fun. There's no need for us to leave together, is there?' Rose squinted at his darkly disapproving expression. 'I know,' she pressed on, 'we came together, in a manner of speaking, but it's not as though we're on a date and there are so many more interesting people I still want to meet.'

'Repeat. Tough. Anyway, don't you think you've had

your fill of interesting people? Or is the entire room interesting after a few glasses of Chablis?'

'Not fair.'

Art shifted uncomfortably, recognising that she had a point. He raked his fingers through his hair and shot her a frowning glance. 'I apologise.' He tugged and undid the bow tie. 'But you've had a few drinks and you're not accustomed to that. I wouldn't feel comfortable leaving you here on your own to get on with the rest of what remains of the evening.'

'Do you think the poor little country girl might end up making a fool of herself? These shoes are killing me, by the way. Are there any chairs around here?'

'I think the poor little country girl might end up finding herself in slightly more hot water than she bargained for. And not many chairs, no. The expectation is for networking, not falling asleep in an armchair.'

'What do you mean about me finding myself in hot water?'

'You're sexy when you get angry.'

Rose blushed and pouted. 'Don't try to change the subject. What do you mean? I'm more than capable of taking care of myself. I've been doing it most of my life.'

'This isn't a quiet, sleepy village in the middle of nowhere.' Art didn't care how this sounded. There was no way he was going to leave her here on her own. The thought of predators circling her, moving in for the kill, made him see red. She was stunning and part of her appeal was the fact that she was so natural, so utterly without pretence, so patently open and honest. Aligned to her intelligence and her dramatic looks...well, it was a recipe for disaster in the big, bad city. If she didn't see that, then it was just as well that she had him around to see it on her behalf.

'I'd noticed, now that you mention it.'

'Have you paid any attention to the number of lechers who have been hanging around you all evening?'

'Have *you*?'

Art flushed. 'You came with me. I can't be blamed for wanting to look out for you.'

Rose's mouth twitched.

Art noted the way her pupils dilated and her eyes widened. He clocked the way her breath hitched and was suddenly turned on in a way that shocked him in its ferocity.

'Should I be grateful?' Rose breathed huskily.

'Don't.'

'Don't what?' The entire roomful of people could have evaporated. There was just the two of them, locked in a bubble in which he was acutely sensitive to every fleeting expression on her face, to the rasping of her breath and the deep, deep longing in her eyes.

'Don't look at me as though you want to touch me. Do that and you're playing with fire.'

'I started playing with fire the minute you came into my life,' Rose said in a tone of complete honesty.

'We should go,' Art told her roughly, leading the way, his hand cupping her elbow.

She was coming on to him. He felt it and, much as he would have liked nothing better than to have followed up on those hot little signals she was giving off, a tipsy Rose wasn't going to do. He wanted her sober and desperate for him, the way he was desperate for her. Nothing else would do.

It was cool and crisp outside and his car was waiting. Art propelled her into it and slid alongside her in the back seat.

'Do you think you have to show me to my door just in case I get waylaid by some of those lecherous men you seem to think are waiting around every corner for a country bumpkin like me?'

'How did you guess?'

'It's the dress. It stands out. When you said that it was going to be smart I had no idea what to buy. I didn't think that everyone would show up in black.'

'I could have warned you. Those functions are usually deadly. Black is an appropriate colour. Anyway, it's not the dress.'

'You don't think so?' Their eyes tangled and she didn't look away. She licked her lips, shivering in the burning intensity of his stare.

'We're here,' Art murmured, relieved.

'So we are. And just when I was beginning to enjoy the car ride.'

'I take it you're enjoying yourself,' he responded once they were out of the car and making their way up to her suite.

'What do you mean?'

'Enjoying playing with me.' Art shot her a wry smile. 'You must know what you're doing to me... I don't play games when it comes to sex...'

'You played a game with me when you slept with me.' She slid the card key into the slot and pushed open the door to her room. When she walked in she didn't push it shut behind her and she didn't tell him that it was fine for him to leave now that he had done the gentlemanly thing and seen her safely to her door. She looked over her shoulder, face serious.

'No game,' Art muttered in a strangled voice. 'The sex was for real. Stop looking at me like that... I'm not going to do anything, Rose. You...you've had a bit to drink. You don't know what you're doing. You don't know what you're playing with.'

'Fire. You've told me that already. I'm playing with fire.' The bed beckoned, oversized, draped in the finest Egyptian cottons and silk.

Rose turned to face him. The lighting in the room was mellow and forgiving. 'I've had a bit to drink,' she admitted without skipping a beat, 'but I'm not the worse for wear. I've been drinking a lot of water in between the wine and I've also eaten for England. Those canapés were to die for.' She walked towards him, kicking off the heels on the way. 'Want me to walk a straight line for you?'

'There's a lot I want you to do for me and walking a straight line doesn't figure.'

'What? What would you like me to do for you? What about this?' She reached down to cup the bulge between his legs and felt his swift intake of breath. Now or never.

Art pressed his hand over hers. He had to because, if he didn't, he wasn't sure what his body was going to do at the pressure she was exerting on his arousal.

'I want you.' Rose maintained eye contact. She'd never seemed more sober. 'When you told me who you really were I felt betrayed and deceived and I never, ever wanted to see you again.' She moved her hand and reached up to link fingers behind his neck. It was as if she'd given herself permission to touch and it was all she wanted to do now. 'I thought that it would be easy to put you behind me. How could I carry on wanting a guy who had used me?'

'Rose...'

'I know you're going to go into a long spiel about why you did what you did but that doesn't matter. What matters is I *couldn't* put you behind me. It didn't matter what you'd done, you'd still managed to get to me in ways...in ways I just never thought possible.'

'You underestimated the power of sex,' Art murmured, resting his hands on her narrow waist.

'I thought that if I saw the real you, the unscrupulous billionaire, then I would be so turned off that this stupid attraction would wither and die.'

Art inclined his head and knew that he had felt something similar, that if he saw her out of her surroundings and in his own terrain then common sense would reassert itself. 'No luck?' He ran his fingers along her back then over her ribcage, leaving them tantalisingly close to her breasts, close enough for her to shiver and half close her eyes.

'It doesn't make sense,' Rose practically wailed.

'Some things don't.' Art hadn't planned on taking her to bed, not tonight. But this wasn't a Rose who was not in control of her faculties. This was a Rose who was so in control that she could vocalise why she was doing what she was doing. This was the Rose he knew—open, honest, forthright and willing to confront a difficult decision head-on.

She couldn't have been a bigger turn-on.

Sex. The power of it. Never more than now was he forced to recognise the strength of body over mind. For someone always in control, this was like being thrown into a raging current without the benefit of a lifebelt. He looked forward to the challenge of battling against that current and emerging the victor.

He hooked his fingers beneath the straps of the sexy red dress and slid them down. She was wearing a silky bra that cupped her breasts like a film of gauze. Art groaned at the sight. The circular discs of her nipples were clearly visible, as was the stiffened bud tipping each pink sphere.

'You gave your phone number to another man,' he said illogically.

'Were you jealous?'

'I wanted to punch him straight into another continent.'

'But you told me I should network...'

'I can't stand the thought of another man touching you.'

'Take me,' she breathed, reaching behind her to unhook the bra, which she shrugged off, stepping back then to unzip the dress at the side and then wriggling out of it so that she was standing in front of him in just her lacy panties.

'Is this the wine talking?' Art was close to the point of no return. She wasn't tripping over her feet but there was no way he was going to get up close and personal with her, only to find himself pushed to one side because she'd fallen asleep on him. He intended to hear groans of pleasure as opposed to the snores of someone who'd had a glass too many.

He smiled at the image because if there was one woman alive who would fall asleep on him it was Rose.

'You're grinning.' Rose began undressing him, clearly trying her best not to rush.

'I'm grinning because I'm busy picturing you falling asleep on me and snoring like a trooper, leaving me with the consolation prize of a cold shower.'

'No chance of that,' Rose said huskily. 'You don't have to worry that I'm under the influence.' She shot him a wicked look from under her lashes. 'Don't tell me that you're so lacking in self-confidence that you think a woman will only sleep with you if she's had one too many.'

'Wench...' But he burst out laughing and propelled her gently back in the direction of the bed, simultaneously completing the job she had begun of getting rid of his clothes. 'Shall I show you how timid and lacking in confidence I am when it comes to pleasuring a woman?'

Rose hit the bed and flopped back onto it, laughing and pulling him down towards her.

'Please,' she breathed, arching up to kiss him. 'Please, please, please... That's exactly what I want...'

CHAPTER NINE

ROSE HAD FANTASISED about those nights when she and
Art had made love. She'd delved deep into her memory
banks and closed her eyes and tasted, in the emptiness
of her bed after he'd disappeared in a puff of treacherous smoke, the touch of his mouth on hers, the feel of
his hands tracing the contours of her body, the heavy
weight of him on top of her and the way her legs had
parted for him, welcoming him into the very core of her.

Now, touching him again, she realised that no
amount of recall could ever have done justice to the
reality of him.

Running her hands over his lean, hard body was like
tasting nectar after a diet of vinegar.

He felt so good.

She traced the corded muscles of his back and then
squirmed so that she was taking charge of proceedings,
flattening him against the bed and angling her body in
such a way that she could devote all her attention to his
vibrant arousal whilst, at the same time, he could pleasure her between her legs.

She'd forgotten how well their bodies meshed, as

though created to fit one against the other. She moved against his questing tongue, her breathing fast and furious, making little guttural noises as she licked and tasted him, feasting on his hardness and playing with his erection while she explored it with her mouth.

Her long hair was everywhere and she flipped it over her shoulder and then arched up, her whole body quivering as ripples of an orgasm began coursing slowly through her.

'Art…' she gasped, not wanting to come.

Not yet.

This time it was Art who took control. With one easy move, he flipped her so that she was now facing him and he edged her up so that there was next to no pause in his ministrations.

She was sitting over him, allowing him the greatest intimacy as he continued to flick his tongue over the stiffened bud of her core. Hands firmly on her waist so that he was keeping her in position, he teased her with his mouth and when her breathing quickened and her body began to stiffen he concentrated on bringing her to a shuddering explosive orgasm.

She spasmed against his mouth and he revelled in the honeyed moistness of her orgasm.

He'd missed this.

He'd missed more than this. It felt so good that he had to reach down and hold his own erection firm because he felt on the very edge of tipping over even though he wasn't inside her, which was where he wanted to be.

Rose subsided, temporarily spent. She lay down next

to him and wrapped her legs over his and, as one, they turned to one another so that their naked bodies were pressed up tight, hot and perspiring.

'Not fair,' she said shakily, but there was a smile in her voice as she wriggled against him, nudging her wetness against his arousal.

'No, it's not,' Art murmured indistinctly. Decidedly unfair that she had this dramatic effect on him, that she was capable of derailing his life the way she had. Just as well that he was putting it back on track. 'Dump the hotel,' he heard himself say, 'and move in with me for the rest of your stay in London.'

'Dump the hotel?'

'It's inconvenient.' He'd never asked any woman to stay in his penthouse apartment but he was comfortable with this decision because a precedent had already been set. He'd shared her space with her so no big deal if she were to share his space with him.

He wanted to be able to reach out and touch her in the middle of the night. He wanted to feel her, warm and aroused, lying next to him. He curved his hand between her thighs and stroked her soft, silky skin, nudging up to feel her wetness graze his knuckles.

He stepped away to fetch a condom from his wallet.

'I guess I could,' Rose murmured as he slipped back into bed to pull her against him. 'I guess it could work...' She parted her legs and sighed as her body began to get excited all over again. 'I mean,' she continued, voice hitched, 'I hadn't banked on any of this happening.'

'That's been the story of my life from the second I saw you,' Art agreed with heartfelt sincerity. 'You may well have converted me to the pleasures of the unforeseen.'

'We both have the same goal.'

Art caressed her breast then levered himself into a position where he could taste it. He flicked his tongue over her nipple and then took it into his mouth so that he could suckle on it while he played with her other nipple, teasing it into tight arousal.

'The same goal...' Her words registered and he slowly kissed his way up to nuzzle against her neck before settling alongside her in a lovely, comfortable position where he could carry on teasing her nipple between his fingers.

'I don't want to want you.' Rose imagined that his next girlfriend might have brains, might have more staying power, might be the woman he let into his life because he had now seen for himself that being in a kitchen to-gether and sharing a meal and then doing the washing-up whilst talking about anything and everything was not something to be feared and reviled. She had done him a favour in pointing him in a different direction and her heart twisted because when he left her behind and walked away it would be into a relationship that might prove to be *the one.*

'And,' she continued, tugging him up because she couldn't focus on anything when he was doing what he'd been doing, 'I know you feel the same.' She paused, a fractional little pause during which he could have jumped in with a denial or said something that might have indicated an interest in more than just *getting her out of his system.* He failed to take the bait. 'So, yes, perhaps if I moved in with you for a couple of days... well, while I'm here, then this thing we have going on... well, we can get it out of our systems faster.'

Art frowned. 'My way of thinking,' he said, on cue. 'There's something about familiarity...'

'You certainly know how to massage a guy's ego. In a minute you'll start comparing me to a virus.'

'Well, it *is* a bit like that.' Rose laughed shakily.

'And what if it doesn't conveniently blow over in a couple of days?'

Rose knew that he was playing devil's advocate. 'It will,' she said firmly. 'We don't have anything in common, Art. We don't have what it takes to have a proper relationship, which is the only thing that would stop this *thing* from blowing over.'

Art frowned. 'Define a *proper* relationship. Is there a checklist for something like that?'

'More or less, if I'm being honest.'

'So now you're saying I tick none of the boxes.'

'There's still one box that gets a very big tick.'

'Glad to hear it.'

'But for me,' Rose said on a sigh, 'a relationship is so much more than just sex.'

'And yet sex, like it or not, is so much a part of any relationship. Too much talking. I get the picture. We're here and this is something we have to do and I can't tell you how much I'm going to enjoy doing it.'

He'd just never mentioned a timeline...

Rose lay in bed, half dozing, drinking him in as he

strolled through the bedroom of his penthouse apartment, completely naked, hunting down his laptop computer because, even though it was still only six in the morning, he was up and ready to work.

She was warm and replete and contented. He'd roused her an hour earlier, nudging her into compliant wakefulness, and they had made love oh, so slowly. Caught in that hazy, half asleep place, Rose had let him take her to places that had left her crying out with pleasure. When, after touching her everywhere, after exploring her soft, warm body, he had finally thrust into her, filling her up, she had felt tears leak down her cheeks and had had to surreptitiously wipe them away because that definitely wasn't part of the deal.

The package deal had kicked off three days previously, when she had fallen into his arms like a starving woman deprived of food who suddenly found herself with a ticket to an all-you-can-eat banquet.

They had made love and then, after a handful of hours' sleep, had made love again and the very next morning she had moved in with him.

They hadn't discussed how long this arrangement was going to last. How did you talk about something like that? How did you work out the length of time it would take for one person to get sick of the other?

How long would it take for him to get bored with her?

Rose knew that that was the way it was going to play out because she wasn't close to getting him out of her system. Indeed, with every passing minute spent together, he became more embedded in her bloodstream.

They'd talked about sex. He did that a lot. When they

made love he would whisper things in her ear that made her whole body burn. He would tell her, in a husky, shaky voice, how much he wanted her and what he wanted to do with her.

He was ruled by lust. He couldn't keep his hands off her and the more he showed that want, the more she needed something more. Something more powerful than *want*.

But that was off the cards and it was always going to be off the cards.

Except…now…looking at him and his careless elegance, Rose felt her heart twist and she knew with an awful sense of despair that she was powerless to initiate the necessary break-up.

She was held in place by something far bigger than lust.

Somehow, against all odds, she had fallen in love with him and she was as powerless now as a speck of flotsam being tossed around this way and that on an unpredictable, fast-flowing current.

She could only make sure he never saw her vulnerability because if he did he would run for the hills.

Love was not on his radar. Not with her. And it never would be. The novelty value that had drawn him to her might not have yet released him from its hold but, now that she was immersed in his life, she knew with dreadful certainty that she was only ever going to be a distraction for him.

He didn't do love. The highs and lows of emotion were things he would seek to avoid. Above everything, he enjoyed the power of control and that included control of his emotional life. He would find someone but she knew in her heart that he would not want someone who was as emotional as she had turned out to be.

Far from being the level-headed woman she'd imagined she was, love had turned her to mush and she wasn't ashamed of it.

Even though she knew that hurt was lurking around the corner, waiting for her.

He produced the laptop from where it had been residing under a bundle of discarded clothes on a chair in his bedroom with a grin of triumph and turned to her. 'First time this hasn't been at my fingertips.'

'You were in a hurry last night.' She forced herself to grin back, keeping it light.

'So I was,' he murmured, dumping the computer and making his way back towards the bed to lean over her, then dropping a kiss on her forehead. 'You do that to me.'

'Make you want to run?' Rose teased, playing with words.

'I can't get to you fast enough.'

Art looked at her for a few serious seconds and Rose had the feeling that there was something he wanted to tell her. A cold chill spread through her but she kept smiling, keeping it light. There could only be one thing he could have wanted to tell her that would have put that serious expression on his face and those words were not ones she wanted to hear. She swallowed down the nasty lump of desperation.

'Stay in bed with me,' she urged. 'Surely work can wait.'

'Not this.' He was still looking at her with that expression on his face.

'Big deal you have to close? I can't imagine there's any deal big enough that you can't ignore it for a few more minutes.'

His expression lightened. 'And to think I've always prided myself on being the kind of guy who can hold out for longer than a couple of minutes…although,' he mused, 'fast and furious does hold a certain appeal, I have to admit.' He sighed, glanced at his cell phone and looked at her again with that pensive expression, thinking thoughts she couldn't begin to fathom. 'Unfortunately, this has nothing to do with work, as such…'

'Why am I getting the feeling that you're speaking in riddles?'

For a few seconds Art remained silent and during those few seconds Rose felt her heart clench tightly, painfully in her chest. Now was the time for her to voice her thoughts and either give him permission to walk away or else pre-empt his departure by announcing hers first.

She was spared any decision because just at that moment his phone buzzed. He looked at the number, then at her.

'Private call,' he said lightly, turning away.

He'd never done that before. Fighting down a wave of nausea, Rose hurriedly leapt out of the bed the second he had left the bedroom, shutting the door quietly behind him. She flew into the bathroom and had a very quick shower. She was dressed and ready for the day and he still had not returned.

Was the call so important that he had to take it at

this ungodly hour, without even taking time out to get dressed?

Was it another woman?

She knew that he had conference calls at strange hours from people in a different time zone, but he had always been fully prepped for those. He'd always conducted them in front of his computer, accessing information while talking to whoever might be on the line.

This was…different.

Rose couldn't credit that he might sleep with her whilst having something going on with someone else. He just wasn't that kind of guy, but then maybe, quite by chance, he had met someone in the last day or so. Was that so tough to believe? Hadn't she already come to the conclusion that he was a changed man, even though he might not see it for himself? A man more open to the possibility of letting someone into his life? A suitable woman.

People gave out vibes without even realising it. Had he projected some sort of availability-to-the-right-woman vibe?

Tense with anxiety, she stood back and looked at her reflection in the mirror. She was nothing special, however much he might wax lyrical about her sexiness.

She was tall and rangy and her looks, such as they were, were unconventional.

Was his private call with a woman with more to offer in the looks department? Was he returning to his comfort zone after his brush with a girl from the wrong side of the tracks?

She found him in the kitchen and he was no longer

on the phone. He was also no longer buck naked but had a towel slung around his lean hips. He must have nabbed it from the spare bathroom while he had been strolling to the kitchen.

Coffee was on the go.

He was so drop-dead gorgeous. So sinfully sexy. So horribly addictive. She remembered that she had fallen for him within five minutes of meeting him. So much for her much-prized defence system when it came to the opposite sex!

'What was that about?'

Art stilled. He'd been reaching for a couple of mugs and he paused for a fraction of a second.

'Coffee?'

'You're not going to answer?'

Rose was dismayed at the shrill, demanding tone of her voice. She had aimed for banter mingled with amused curiosity. She had ended up with shrewish nag but she couldn't claw her way back from the question and she wasn't sure she wanted to. If he was going to break it off with her because of some other woman then he should have the decency to come right out and tell her.

She shouldn't have to second-guess.

'I didn't think that sharing my private phone calls was part and parcel of what we had.'

Rose flushed. 'Who was it?' she was horrified to hear herself ask.

'I think this is a conversation best put on hold,' Art said coolly.

'And I happen to think that I deserve an answer. If it was a personal call with another woman, then I deserve to know. I realise this isn't anything serious but I'm not interested in sleeping with anyone who's seeing someone else on the side.'

'Is that what you think?' he asked quietly.

Rose hesitated but, like someone who had crossed a certain line, she was now doomed to carry on walking that road. And besides, she roused herself to a place of self-righteous justification, she *did* deserve to know if he was thinking about ditching her for someone else!

'How do I know what to think if you won't tell me what's going on?' she muttered.

'I'm going to get changed.'

'You're walking away from an uncomfortable conversation,' she challenged but he was already heading back to the bedroom and after a while she tripped along behind him.

Art stopped dead in his tracks and looked at her, eyes flint-hard. 'I don't do this,' he said calmly.

Rose returned that gaze with one that was equally cool. 'Do what, Art?' She folded her arms, determined to brave out what she knew was going to be their final conversation. 'Discuss anything you might find a little awkward? I know this isn't about love and commitment, but it should be about respect and if you respected me you wouldn't baulk at having this conversation.'

Rose hoped that he would read nothing in her eyes that gave the lie to that statement because when it came to love she was drowning under the weight of it. Pride would never allow her to admit that, however. She was going to leave but she would leave without him ever having cause to think that he had had a narrow escape from yet another needy woman who had foolishly disobeyed his *Do Not Trespass* signs and developed unacceptable feelings towards him.

He had let slip in conversation the headaches he had had with a couple of previous girlfriends who had wanted him to meet the parents, who had mentioned the possibility of making plans further ahead than the next couple of hours.

Rose had absorbed those passing comments and was not going to be bracketed in the same category, to become yet another irritating ex to be produced during some future conversation with some future woman.

Art's eyebrows shot up but something made him hesitate before heading back to the bedroom.

'I'm not going to have this conversation,' he said abruptly. 'If you feel that I am the sort of man who disrespects women, who has somehow disrespected *you*, then it's clear that we should not be together.'

'Art...'

'I'll be back but don't wait up.'

'Is that your way of saying that you'd like me to be gone by the time you return? Because if it is then why don't you have the guts to come right out and say so?'

'No one speaks to me like that!'

Rose folded her arms and stared at him mutinously. On the inside she was breaking up into pieces. On the outside she refused to show him just how much she was hurting. 'Then you're right,' she said gruffly. 'It's clear that we shouldn't be together if I'm only allowed to speak to you in a certain way!'

The tense silence between them stretched on and on and on…stretched until she could feel all her wretchedness washing over her in a painful tidal wave.

'Like I said,' Art drawled, 'don't wait up.'

Rose watched in silence as he threw aside the towel to get dressed. She found that she couldn't look at him. Even at the height of this toxic argument, she could still be moved by his sheer animal beauty. She didn't want to be moved.

He left the room without a backward glance and for a while she actually hoped that he would have second thoughts and return.

He didn't.

She had no idea where he'd gone and her feverish imagination provided her with all sorts of unwelcome scenarios. Had he disappeared into the waiting arms of some other woman? Had he somehow manoeuvred a situation in which she would react in a way that would give him an out?

She wasn't going to hang around to find out and there was nothing more to be said.

She gathered her things in record time. She hadn't brought much with her and what little she *had* brought took ten minutes to toss into her case.

She paused to look at the wonderful dress she had worn for the charity event that had been so memorable for so many reasons.

No way was she taking it with her.

It took her half an hour and then she was out of the mansion block and casting one last look behind her from the back of a black cab.

* * *

Art returned to an empty apartment. Of course he knew that she would be gone by the time he got back. He'd disappeared for over four hours. No explanation. What would have possessed her to hang around?

He flipped on the lights and went straight to his computer and switched it on. In his peripheral vision, he could tell that all her belongings had gone with her. There was no need for him to waste his energy hunting for evidence of her departure.

The screen opened up and he stared at it and realised that it really was possible to look at numbers and letters and symbols and see absolutely nothing whatsoever.

She would have caught a taxi to the station and would be heading back to her house by train. He was tempted to look up the possible departure times of the trains and resisted.

He'd done the right thing. That reaction was sufficient to harden his resolve. He had been weak once, had engineered a situation because he had still wanted her and had been unable to resist the demands of his body, but that weakness was something that had to be overcome.

He had seen where emotional weakness could lead. Those lessons had been learned when he had been too young but they were lessons he would never forget.

His indecision had been getting on his nerves and so he'd killed it fast. He hadn't signed up to a querulous woman throwing a hissy fit because he refused to be subjected to a cross-examination.

So what if that phone call had had nothing to do with a woman?

He scowled, mood plummeting faster than the speed of light. Right about now she should be winding her arms around him, warm and naked and distracting.

Right about now he should be forgetting about work and climbing right back into bed with her because he couldn't do anything *but* climb into bed with her whenever they were in this room.

Art envisaged what her reaction would be in a couple of months, when the full extent of that phone call became common knowledge.

He'd deceived her once but she had returned to him and he knew that it had been something she would not have undertaken lightly.

Sex was all well and good but she would have had to square it with her conscience and he'd never met any woman with a more lively conscience. Her conscience practically bounced off the walls.

To discover what she inevitably would, to find out without benefit of any explanation...

He abandoned all attempts to focus on work, sat back and wearily rubbed his eyes with the pads of his thumbs.

He'd never thought himself to have a particularly active or vivid imagination but he was imagining now, in a very vivid fashion indeed, the horror that would engulf her were she to discover, as she would in due course, that there would be more going on that vast acreage of land than a handful of tasteful houses.

It would be the ultimate deception for her because she would know that he would have had countless opportunities to raise the issue. To be deceived once was forgivable. To be deceived twice would be the ultimate sin in her eyes.

He should have broached the subject. That phone call would have provided the perfect opportunity to raise it. Instead, the shutters had slammed shut on her. Habit. He had never been a man to be nagged or cajoled into saying or doing anything he didn't want to say or do. He had reacted with stunning predictability.

And it had been a mistake.

The truth was that she deserved honesty—and that was exactly what he was going to give her.

The slate would then be wiped clean.

Mind made up, Art didn't bother consulting anything as pedestrian as train timetables. Why would he? He had two options. His private helicopter or his driver. Or he could take any one of his fast cars and drive himself.

Which was exactly what he chose to do.

He didn't know whether he would reach her house before her but it didn't matter. What mattered, and mattered with an urgency he couldn't quite put into words, was that they talked.

He'd say what he had to say and then leave.

Traffic was light as he left London. A Ferrari was built to eat up the miles with silent efficiency and it did.

Under normal circumstances, he would have kicked back and enjoyed the dynamic horsepower of a car he rarely got to drive but his mind was too busy projecting the conversation that was going to take place.

He made it to her house in record time and knew, without even having to ring the doorbell, that she wasn't yet there.

With any luck, she was going to show up soon and hadn't decided to do a spot of sightseeing before catching the train back.

Art positioned the powerful car at the perfect angle to see her just as she entered her drive. He wasn't going to let her run away this time.

Rose was spent by the time she made it to the local out-post where trains arrived in their own sweet time. The slow journey would have got on her nerves at any other time but on this occasion she relished the unhurried tempo of the trip. Her head felt as though it was burst-ing with thoughts, too many thoughts to be contained, just as her heart was bursting with too many feelings.

And at the very centre of all those thoughts and feel-ings was the dark, throbbing knowledge that she was not going to see Art again. The void that opened up in-side her when she thought about that was so big that it threatened to swallow her up like a sinkhole.

At the station she hailed a taxi, which exited the small car park as though urgency was a concept that didn't exist. She knew the taxi driver. She had done some pro bono work for his father two years previ-ously, and she heard herself chatting to him but from a long way away.

She was so tired.

Lapsing into silence, she closed her eyes and wasn't aware that she was approaching her house until the taxi began to slow, until it swerved slowly into the drive, and only then did she open her eyes and stir herself into wakefulness.

Only then did she see the red car in the drive, sleek and elegant and so, *so* sexy.

CHAPTER TEN

ART WAS OUT of the car before the passenger door of the taxi had opened. He'd been hanging around for over an hour. He'd stretched his legs a couple of times but he still felt cramped and restless.

Watching through narrowed eyes as she emerged, he felt at peace for the first time since he had left London.

No…since she had re-entered his life, if not before.

His thoughts were so clear he felt washed clean.

He could see the wariness in her eyes and he strode towards her before that wariness could persuade her to get back into the taxi and disappear, leaving him stranded on her doorstep.

'What are you doing here?' Rose's voice was curt as she paid the taxi driver, who was watching proceedings with keen interest. 'Thanks, Stephen—' she said to the driver through the window of the car, eyebrows raised '—I won't keep you. I expect Jenny and the kids would like to have you home.'

'That the big-shot she's been banging on about for weeks?'

'No idea, Steve. I don't know how many big-shots

Jenny's met recently...' She slammed shut the door and leaned towards him. 'Give her my love and the thumbs-up that everything's in place for the changes to the library. She can start picking out colours for the new kids' space.'

Rose was playing for time but, with no distraction left, she remained where she was as Steve headed away. Her case was on the ground at her feet.

'I've been waiting here for over an hour.' For the first time in living memory, Art was nervous. He almost failed to recognise the sensation. He couldn't take his eyes off her. He wanted to climb into her head and read what she was thinking but her expression was cool and remote and he wondered...where did he go from here?

Scowling and ill at ease, he walked towards her and was pleased to note that, almost indiscernibly, she flinched. He was having some kind of effect on her and that was good because, going by her expression, he could have been a wind-up toy.

'So sorry to have kept you waiting,' Rose said coolly, tilting her head at a mutinous angle and refusing to back away. 'And you still haven't told me what you're doing here.'

'I...' He shook his head, looked away, raked his fingers through his hair and then returned his dark gaze to her pale, cool face. 'I...shouldn't have...let you leave... with the wrong idea...' was pretty much all he could find to say.

'Not interested,' Rose muttered, looking away. 'You're a free agent and you can do what you want. You're right. You don't owe me any explanations.'

'Are we going to carry on this conversation out here?'

'I didn't think we were having a conversation. You came here to explain whatever it is you feel you should explain and I'm liberating you from that responsibility. So there's no conversation to be had.'

'It was about the land.'

'Sorry?'

'I was on the phone to someone about the land. The land you were protecting from greedy developers like me. I wanted to tell you…' Art looked away but only momentarily.

'The land?' Rose looked at him in confusion because this was the last thing she'd been expecting to hear. 'You weren't on the phone to a woman?'

'I'm monogamous.' His lips quirked in a dry smile but he had no idea how this was going to play out and the smile only lasted a second. His usual panache and easy self-assurance were nowhere in evidence. 'And when would I have had time to think about frolicking with another woman? You've kept me pretty busy…'

'What about the land?'

Lengthening silence greeted this and eventually Rose spun around and began walking towards the house.

'Tell me you haven't been keeping more from me about the land,' she said quietly as soon as the front door was shut behind them. She clearly hadn't wanted to invite him into the house but he'd left her with no choice.

'You don't have the complete picture,' Art said flatly. Cold dread was gripping him and he knew now that full disclosure should have been his approach. But events had moved swiftly and now…

He was going to lose her and if that happened he had

no idea what he was going to do because he couldn't contemplate a life without her in it. He'd screwed up.

'Start small, end up big. Is that the complete picture?' They were in the kitchen. Rose felt as if she could do with a stiff drink but instead she began the business of making herself a cup of coffee—anything to still her nerves, which were running amok as she gradually worked out that he had deceived her once again.

Had he slept with her the second time round so that he could build up to yet more revelations about what he intended to do with the acres of land he had bought?

Had he sweet-talked her into phase one with the intention of sweet-talking her into phase two, except she'd scuppered his plans by overhearing that conversation, jumping to the wrong conclusion and then walking out on him before he could complete what he had set out to do?

She felt sick.

'You didn't want a handful of tasteful mansions with lots of spare land, did you? That wouldn't have made financial sense. What you wanted was to start with a handful of tasteful mansions and then what, Art? A housing estate? Mass housing that would mean more profits for you? As if you aren't rich enough already.'

She managed to make it to the kitchen table, now free from placards and posters and cardboard with rousing slogans, and she sank into one of the chairs.

'Way too rich.' Art drew a chair up close to hers, as if to stop her from somehow fleeing the room. She didn't like his positioning and automatically drew back into herself, freezing him out as her defences came down. When he leaned forward, elbows resting loosely on his thighs, he was practically touching her.

'Too rich to think about whether putting up a hundred houses is going to net me more money than putting up ten.' He sighed heavily, caught her eye and held her gaze. 'But you're right. I haven't been entirely honest with you.'

'I don't want to hear.'

'And normally that would work for me,' Art returned. 'Normally justifying myself in any way, shape or form isn't something I would see the need to do, but in this instance...'

'Am I supposed to think that you have a conscience?' Rose questioned painfully.

'I don't suppose I've given you a lot of reason to trust anything I have to say.'

'Spot on.'

'But...' He shook his head. 'I'll try to start at the beginning. I... You'll have to bear with me. I don't... know how this is done.'

'How what is done?'

'This talking business.'

'This *talking business*? What does that even *mean*?' But there was an air of vulnerability about him that she'd never seen before and it did something to her even though she fought hard to resist the pull and tried to remember that this wasn't going to end up in a good place.

'I... I've never had much time for talking, Rose. Not when it came to women. When it came to women, things were very clear-cut. It was all about mutual pleasure.

Nothing lasted and nothing was meant to. It was the way I liked it. When I met you, I had an agenda, but in no way was sleeping with you part of that agenda, and of course that should have set the alarm bells ringing. The fact that sleeping with you made no sense and yet I had to do it, had to get you into bed. It was as though something bigger and stronger than me had taken charge and was dictating how I behaved when it came to you.'

Rose looked at him with a jaundiced expression and wondered whether she was supposed to melt at that admission. She wished he'd back away a bit. His proximity was suffocating her.

'You need to just tell me what else you've been hiding from me,' she said quietly. 'I don't want to hear about…how much you wanted me…'

Art sat back and half closed his eyes, then he looked at her for a while in silence.

'There was always an agenda for that land. I had to have it. Had to make sure that everything went through and I had to get the residents of the village onside. Yes, for the expensive houses that were going to be built but also, in due course, for more building work that I had planned.'

'I thought as much.' Rose looked away, heart pounding, bile in her mouth.

'You really don't.' He turned her face to his, finger lightly under her chin, compelling them to lock eyes, and Rose gazed helplessly at him.

'I can't bear the thought of being used, Art. All my life, the one thing I've taken away from what happened to my mum is that I would never allow myself to be used by any man. She abandoned me for a man she met and knew for five seconds! Yes, she came back but I'd lost a lot in that time that she'd been away and I'd grown up and learned lessons. Lesson one was that when it came to my heart, common sense was always going to be more valuable than stupid, crazy *lust.*'

'We're singing from the same song sheet,' Art murmured. 'We both had lessons ingrained into us thanks to our backgrounds. Rich or poor, our experiences made us the cautious people we ended up being. I was happy to be ruled by lust. I just resisted anything more than that. Until you. Until you came along.'

'What do you mean?' Rose found that she was holding her breath and she exhaled slowly, hoping that her calm, detached exterior was still in place, making no assumptions even though her heart was beating fast now but with forbidden excitement.

'I told myself that it was a mistake to sleep with you. I didn't want the waters to be muddied. I had come for a specific reason and I naturally assumed that a minor temptation wasn't going to confuse the issue. How wrong I was. I decided where was the harm? There wouldn't be any fallout because I was always, had always been and always would be, in control of my choices. We were both consenting adults and, if anything, getting you into bed would give me an added advantage in persuading you to listen to reason when it came to the protest.' She looked away sharply and Art tilted her stubborn face back to his.

'The truth of the matter was that I couldn't resist you. You did something to me and you carried on doing it even when I left and returned to London. I couldn't get you out of my mind. I kept drifting off into inappropriate fantasies at inappropriate times. In the middle of conversations, in the thick of an important meeting, just as I was about to sink my teeth into the finest food money could buy. And yet I still didn't wake up to what should have been blindingly obvious.'

'Which is what?'

'Somewhere along the line I fell in love with you. Please don't say anything because I need to tell you about the land. After you've heard what I have to say I'll leave, but I felt you needed to know...how I felt.'

'Art...'

He'd fallen in love with her? Did he really mean that?

Her heart had migrated to her mouth so when she spoke her voice was muffled and she had to clear her throat. 'Do you mean that?'

'I wasn't looking for love. I've never been looking for love. My father had so many ex-wives that so-called *love* was always in plentiful supply and always, without fail, ended up in the divorce courts, where each and every one would wrangle until they went blue in the face for a slice of his money. I was jaded beyond belief by the time I left my teens behind. Love was for idiots and I was never going to be an idiot. The truth is that I just never fell in love and I never realised that love makes idiots of us all.'

'Why didn't you say something?' Rose whispered.

'How could I,' Art asked wryly, 'when I didn't recognise the symptoms?'

Symptoms? Never had that single word held such thrilling promise.

'Please tell me about the land.' Everything should have been perfect. The man of her dreams had just declared his love for her and yet the rest of his story cast a long shadow, even though she couldn't see what could possibly spoil the moment. She just knew that a fly in the ointment could turn out to be a lot more toxic than it might first appear. If she was going to get toxic, then she wanted to get it straight away.

'I targeted that land because I want to build an equestrian centre there,' Art said heavily. 'And not just an equestrian centre, but something of a farming complex. You won't be getting the neat arrangement of polite, high-spec houses you signed up for and there's no other way of putting it but to tell it like it is.' His mouth twisted crookedly. 'In hindsight, if I could have predicted how circumstances would unravel, I would have taken the plunge from the very start but hindsight, as I've discovered to my cost, is a wonderful thing. And, like I've said—' he smiled with self-mockery '—hindsight isn't something I've ever had time for. My predictive talents had never been challenged and when you know what's coming you're not glancing over your shoulder and shaking your head because you took the wrong turning.'

'Sorry? You want to build *a farm*?' Rose was finding it hard to get past that stark announcement.

'Long story, but… I have a stepbrother, José. He's severely autistic and currently in a home in the New

Forest. He's not yet twenty-two but the home, good as it is, really can't deal with the needs of a young adult.'

'You have a brother...'

'Stepbrother. And the only step-sibling I've ever had time for. Ironic, given his mother had very *little* time for him. In fact, my father had no idea he existed at all until after the marriage had ended. Eliza kept her son's existence under wraps, just in case it jeopardised the pot of gold at the end of the rainbow. At the time, José had been shoved in a mixed bag home and practically forgotten. I met him and felt sorry for him. No, more than that. I wanted to protect him and then I grew to love him. He was honest and trusting and incredibly talented in certain areas but he'd been hung out to dry by his scheming mother, who had no time for him. To her credit, she did pop her head into the home now and again but where she left off, I found that I was taking over. Years after she disappeared from my father's life, she was killed in a road accident, at which point I took José under my wing. I was climbing the ladder of success. It became my mission to ensure that he got the best that money could buy. I saved José but, in a strange way, I think José also saved me.'

'Art, my head is spinning.'

'There's no concise way to explain all of this. I just need you to understand that my dilemma was finding a place where I could develop a centre for José and for other kids like him. A handful. He is soothed by horses and enjoys being outdoors. He has a way with them. The farm would be something of a therapeutic centre.

Some arts and crafts could be incorporated. You'd be surprised at how talented some of these kids are.'

'But why on earth didn't you say anything about this?'

'To the council?' His eyebrows shot up. 'People can be strange when it comes to having anyone different as their neighbours. It took a long time to find a suitable location, somewhere commutable for me, a convenient middle ground for other occupants. I wasn't going to risk jeopardising the project by introducing it from the beginning. I thought that by the time the community got accustomed to the notion of the land being developed they would be more open to my future plans for the place.'

'I love you,' Rose said simply, because all of this showed her a side to him that she'd known was there, a caring, thoughtful side lurking underneath the ruthless billionaire exterior.

It was the side that had sucked her in and, even when he'd confessed to his deception, had kept her sucked in because deep down she had known him for the good guy he was. She'd seen the moral integrity underneath the tough *love is for the birds* exterior.

'You're not upset that I lied to you yet again?' Art looked as though his heart was soaring.

'I'd like to meet your stepbrother one day.'

Art reached out but he didn't tug her towards him. Instead, he held her hands in his. It was a chaste gesture that made her smile.

'You will,' he said gruffly. 'But first you have to promise me one thing.'

'What?' She nudged closer to him and played with his fingers. She couldn't help herself. She reached out and stroked the side of his face with the back of her hand, then she traced the contours of his mouth.

She leaned into him and kissed him, a slow, tender, melting kiss and it felt good to have her love out in the open, to be as vulnerable as he was.

'Promise me that you'll marry me,' Art said in a muffled voice. 'Because I can't imagine a life without you in it. I want to go to sleep with you and wake up to you. I don't want to ever let you go.'

'Yes.' Rose smiled. 'A thousand times *yes.*'

They were married just as the finishing touches were being put to the local library.

It had been planned as a quiet wedding but it turned out to be rather larger than either of them had expected. Once one person had been invited others had to be included, and Rose discovered that she had done a lot more for the residents of her quiet community than she had ever dreamed.

Everyone wanted to come.

Everyone knew her story and the wedding was almost as much of a fairy tale for them as for her.

She wore a simple cream dress and little silk buds were woven into her long hair, and the look on Art's face when he turned to look at her as she walked up the aisle of the little country church was something she would take with her for as long as she lived.

And now...

Six months later, life couldn't be better and so much had changed. For starters, the house had no more leaks in need of fixing. It had been renovated to its original splendour but, with all the right planning permission in place, was now a fully functioning office catering for several start-up companies as well as the legal practice which Phil, Rose's partner, had taken over in its entirety.

Rose no longer lived there but whenever she returned she marvelled at its wonderful transformation.

'I don't think,' she confided to Art a few weeks after she had moved out and shortly before their wedding, 'that I ever really saw it as *my* house. Even though, technically, it was. And even though I always, always knew it to be a real blessing. I guess I always somehow associated it with a time in my life that brought back bad memories so, whilst I'm happy it's renovated, I'm pleased I no longer live in it.'

Where she lived now could not have been more wonderful. Not the sprawling modernist vision in London which Art had occupied but, he also admitted, never actually viewed as anything other than a handy space in a useful location, but a country cottage that was the perfect blend of ancient and modern.

It was just outside London, convenient for commuting both back to London by train and to the centre in the Cotswolds where José would be eventually located.

Rose had fallen in love with the cottage at first sight.

With the husband of her dreams and the house to match, she hadn't thought that life could get any better but it had.

She started as she heard the front door open and her heart quickened, as it always did at the arrival of her husband.

She rose to greet him and smiled at the naked love and desire etched on his lean face.

He was so beautiful and he was *hers*. She smiled at the thrill of possession that swelled inside her.

Art smiled back, moving smoothly towards her while undoing the top couple of buttons of his shirt.

'You don't get to look like that without accepting that there'll be consequences.' He pulled her towards him, cupped her rounded bottom and crushed her against him so that she could feel the tell-tale stirring of his desire.

'Look like what?' Rose burst out laughing, drawing back and capturing his face between her hands.

'Oh, you know…pair of jeans, tee shirt, flip-flops…'

'Oh, you mean my *fancy* outfit.'

'You've gone all out on the dinner, I see.' Art peered around her to see the kitchen table, which was candlelit and set in some style. 'What have I forgotten? It's not a birthday and it's definitely not our anniversary, unless it's the anniversary of the first time you decided that I was the best thing that ever happened to you, which would have been, hmm, about five minutes after we met?'

'Time's done nothing to dim that ego of yours, Arturo da Costa, has it?'

Art burst out laughing. 'Don't keep me in suspense. With any other woman, I'd be inclined to think that you're bracing me for some wildly extravagant purchase, but then, my darling, you're not any other woman and I thank my lucky stars for that every day.'

Rose tugged him into the huge open-plan kitchen with its granite countertops and its wonderful state-of-the-art built-in appliances.

'Champagne,' Art murmured, glancing at the counter. 'Now I'm really beginning to get worried.'

'Then don't. I actually would have dressed up for the occasion but I opted for comfortable over glamorous.'

'Don't distract me.'

'The champagne is for you. I'll be sticking to mineral water for the moment and for the next, oh, let's say… nine months or so…'

'Are you telling me what I think you're telling me?'

'I'm pregnant.'

Art wrapped his arms around her and held her tight to him for several long minutes. 'I couldn't have asked for a better end to my day, my darling. I love you so very much.'

'And I love you too. Now and for ever.'

* * * * *

LET'S TALK
Romance

For exclusive extracts, competitions
and special offers, find us online:

- **f** facebook.com/millsandboon
- ⊙ @millsandboonuk
- 🐦 @millsandboon

Or get in touch on 0844 844 1351*

For all the latest titles coming soon,
visit millsandboon.co.uk/nextmonth

Want even more
ROMANCE?

Join our bookclub today!

'Mills & Boon books, the perfect way to escape for an hour or so.'

Miss W. Dyer

'Excellent service, promptly delivered and very good subscription choices.'

Miss A. Pearson

'You get fantastic special offers and the chance to get books before they hit the shops'

Mrs V. Hall

Visit millsandbook.co.uk/Bookclub and save on brand new books.

MILLS & BOON